# INDIA
## *Now and Through Time*

CATHERINE ATWATER GALBRAITH
and
RAMA MEHTA

*Illustrated with photographs and a map*

HOUGHTON MIFFLIN COMPANY
BOSTON

*Frontispiece: Gate of temple at Srirangam, Trichinopoly, South India*

PICTURE CREDITS

Ishar Beri, 2, 3, 4, 6, 8 (bottom), 17, 18 (right), 20, 21 (above), 26, 32, 37, 40 (right), 42, 44, 45, 60, 68, 89, 90, 101, 108, 115, 125, 127 (bottom), 129, 134, 135, 138, 141; Stuart French & Bonnie Kreps, 9, 21 (center), 23, 24, 53, 128, 131; Catherine Atwater Galbraith, 10 (right), 12, 19, 27, 41, 49, 54, 66, 67, 72, 132, 133; John Kenneth Galbraith, 18 (left), 33; Goras Studios, 74; Government of India Department of Tourism and the Information Bureau, New Delhi, and Consul General Ahuja and staff, New York, frontispiece, 7, 8 (above), 10 (left), 21 (bottom), 22, 29, 30, 34, 38, 40 (left), 47, 50, 62, 77, 78-79, 80, 81, 83, 84, 85, 93, 96, 102, 103, 117, 118, 122, 123, 124, 127 (above), 137, 140; India House Library, London, 113; Rama Mehta, 16; Ismail Merchant & James Ivory, 35; Museum of Fine Arts, Boston, 57, 76, 97; Victoria & Albert Museum, London, 39, 69, 95, 99, 105, 107.

Library of Congress Cataloging in Publication Data

Galbraith, Catherine Atwater.
  India, now and through time.

  Bibliography: p.
  Includes index.
  SUMMARY: Introduces the land, history, culture, and people of the country with the second highest population in the world.
    1. India – Juvenile literature. [1. India] I. Mehta, Rama, joint author. II. Title.
DS407.G26   1980     954     80-11591
ISBN 0-395-29207-7

HAL  10 9 8 7 6 5 4

# Contents

*In memory of Connie*

*To Averell, with love*


*For Rama, in gratitude*

*for her friendship*

# Foreword

In May 1961 Vice President and Mrs. Lyndon B. Johnson, President
John F. Kennedy's sister Jean with her husband Stephen Smith, and
two full planes of government officials and journalists stopped off
in Delhi in the course of a quick trip around the world. This was
our first state visit, my husband having just become the United
States Ambassador to India. One day was allowed for sightseeing
—all visitors must pay their respects to the Taj Mahal. For the oc-
casion I needed the most knowledgeable guide I could find, and it
was easily agreed that this person was Rama Mehta. In addition
to all else, she was a former Indian foreign service officer; her husband, Jagat Mehta, was a high officer in the Ministry of External
Affairs. The Johnsons did not have a great deal of time for Indian
history but in those few hours with Rama I learned much.

After my husband returned to teach at Harvard and we moved
back to Cambridge, Massachusetts, from New Delhi, Rama Mehta
was twice a fellow at the Radcliffe Institute for Independent
Study. In May 1967, at the end of her second appointment at the
Institute, we decided to write together a book that would describe
India as we knew it—one born and brought up there, the other a
newcomer from the West. Since we would soon be half a world
apart, we divided the labor—Rama would do the research and I
the writing. The first-person observations are usually mine. In the
autumn of 1968 Rama, with her daughter Vijay, and I traveled in
Rajasthan all the way to the distant desert capital of Jaisalmer,
where we stayed in a dusty dak bungalow, the only shelter then
available for visitors, and brought our bedrolls and peanut butter,

v

cheese, tea and warm Coca-Cola, which we had for breakfast, lunch, and dinner for three wonderful days. When I mention this trip, *we* means both of us.

In our writing I would think of matters a foreigner might want explained—what spices go into *pan*—which an Indian would take for granted. Aerograms went back and forth. But since mail to India is slow, I sometimes turned to other knowledgeable friends who were conveniently nearby—Dorothy Dahl; Dr. M. S. Rand-hawa, the great authority on Indian painting; Bimla Nanda Bissell, my longtime associate in India; Ambassador L. K. Jha in Washington; and Vijay Mehta, all of whom gave guidance; and to my sternest critic, John Kenneth Galbraith, without whom I might never have known India at all. He also came to my rescue in selecting the pictures from among hundreds and allowed his talented staff, headed by Andrea Williams, to prepare the manuscript. Emily G. Wilson helped, as ever, at home.

We took some of the pictures ourselves. Others were provided by the Government of India Department of Tourism and the Press Information Bureau, New Delhi, particularly by Mr. H. S. Gupte; by Consul General Ahuja and the Indian consulate staff in New York; by the Victoria and Albert Museum and the India House Library in London; by Juliana Boyd of the Museum of Fine Arts in Boston; by Ismail Merchant and James Ivory, Stuart French and Bonnie Kreps, Norman Dahl, and especially by Ishar Beri, the talented photographer of the United States embassy in New Delhi. To all I continue to be most grateful.

*India Now and Through Time* was first published in September 1971. I saw my first copy on my way back from visiting the Mehtas in Tanzania, where Jagat Mehta was Indian High Commissioner, soon to return to New Delhi as Foreign Secretary. I was not in India after 1975, and there were disturbing reports about Rama's health. Meanwhile much was happening and we thought of preparing a new edition of our book. On June 7, 1978, Rama died of a massive heart attack.

I decided to revise the book on my own. Most changes are in

the last chapter, although I have made small revisions as needed throughout. Once again I am indebted to my husband and his staff, notably Rosamaria Toruño for her typing, and to wise and informed friends—to L. K. Jha, now Governor of Kashmir, to Mrs. Vijaya Lakshmi Pandit, and above all to the Mehta family for their encouragement and help. Ambassador to Switzerland Gurbachan Singh provided me with material last winter and Ambassador N. A. Palkhivala supplied me with facts, figures and the assistance of Mr. Harsh K. Bhasin of the Indian embassy in Washington. My appreciation and gratitude go to them all.

The first edition was dedicated to the late Dean Constance E. Smith at the Radcliffe Institute and to Averell Harriman, who, more than anyone, pressed me to complete it. This edition has a further dedication—to Rama.

Rama Mehta was as at home in New Delhi as she was in the seclusion of the haveli in Udaipur—or in Peking, Dar es Salaam, or Harvard. Traditional values and social change, especially for Indian women, were her passionate concern. Three hours in her company would pass in a moment, brightened by her whole-hearted enjoyment of discussion, her sharp comments, her laughter and wit. I could not have had a more luminous and perceptive interpreter of Indian life and customs. Wherever she was, she left devoted friends. I am one of them.

*Catherine Atwater Galbraith*

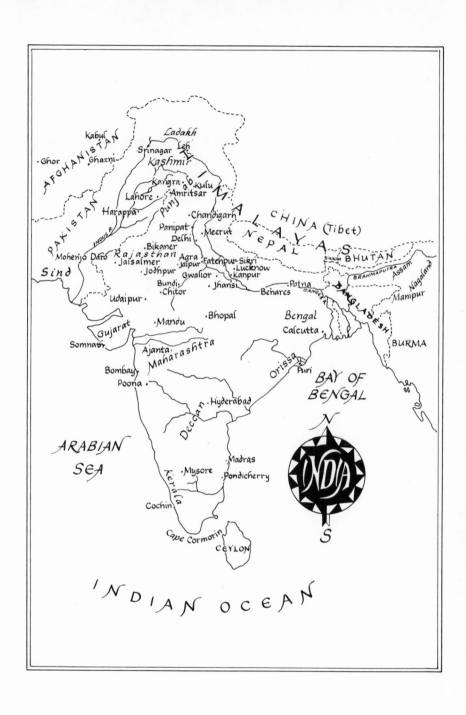

# 1
## Where Is India?
## What Is the Country Like?

On the map of Asia, India looks like a kite, jutting south into the Indian Ocean until the narrow tip almost touches Ceylon, while the top reaches the Chinese border. The crossbars of the kite stretch over Bangladesh to Burma on the right and on the left to Pakistan. New Delhi, the capital of India, is slightly above the point at which the bars would meet. North of India, in the arc between Iran and Burma, are Afghanistan, the Soviet Union and China. West, beyond the sea, is Africa. To the east are Thailand, Malaysia and the islands of Indonesia.

The countries of Central Asia are separated from the Indian subcontinent (this includes Pakistan, Bangladesh, Ceylon, Bhutan, Nepal and tiny Sikkim, since 1975 a part of India) by the Himalayas, the tallest mountains in the world. Some are almost five miles high, twice the height of the highest mountains in Europe. The first time I flew over them was in the nose of a military aircraft. I knew then that I was seeing thousands of miles of peaks and crevasses that had never been seen by anyone until there were high altitude airplanes and that no one could ever traverse on foot. A few passes offer a way over small parts of this wilderness, for men carrying headloads, or with yaks and sturdy ponies, but they are so high that they are snowbound most of the year. Old trade routes to China are to the east. The Japanese in World War II reached this edge of India and near here the Chinese attacked

1

*Himalayan wilderness—flying to Leh from Delhi in a C 130. Peaks near Leh include K2 (28,261 feet).*

in 1962. Again, at the western end of the Himalayas the passes through the mountains are wider and easier to cross. In olden times, nomadic tribes and foreign armies reached India's fertile plains by these routes.

Below the mountains (the lower part of the kite), India is bounded west and east by the Arabian Sea, the Bay of Bengal and the Indian Ocean. At the southern point these waters meet. On the coasts are many harbors, on some of which are now such large cities as Bombay, Calcutta and Madras. India has long traded with her neighbors by sea. The sea has also brought travelers from Europe, including, by legend, St. Thomas, and, later on, Christian missionaries who settled in the south of India as early as the sixth century. In 1498, six years after Columbus discovered America while looking for a sea route to the Indies, the Portuguese explorer Vasco da Gama found one by sailing from Europe around Africa. The name "India" was probably given by the Greeks. It is derived from the Sindhu, i.e., the river Indus, along which India's first civilization developed. Hindus called their land Bharata Varsha, the land of Bharata, a legendary king.

India, one-third the area of the United States, is the seventh largest country in the world. From north to south is approximately 2000 miles; east to west, at the widest point, is over 1800 miles. Calcutta is almost as far from Bombay as New York is from Little Rock, Arkansas. In population, about 650 million, India is second only to China. It has as many people as there are in all of Africa and South America combined. Four-fifths of the population

*Tea gardens, near Darjeeling*

*Crossing the Brahmaputra*

of India live in the villages, nearly 600,000 of them.* With so many people, even in remote places it is hard to be alone.

Within sight of the towering snow-covered Himalaya Mountains are terraced rice fields, apricot and apple orchards, or neatly clipped tea bushes. Forests of deodars, like California redwoods, and rhododendrons, climb to the bare rocks. Stately chenar trees, which resemble a huge maple or a giant oak, shade the parks. Abruptly then, the large foothills end in broad plains through which flow three great rivers—the Indus, the Ganges, the Brahmaputra—with their tributaries. They are very long: from its source in the Himalayas, the Ganges runs 1,540 miles eastward to the Bay of Bengal, and the other two rivers are even longer. Cities have grown on their banks and tributaries, including Agra and Delhi, and Benares, the holiest city of the Hindus. The rivers of

* According to the 1971 census there are 575,936 villages and 2643 towns and cities. (*India.* A Reference Annual 1977–78. Ministry of Information and Broadcasting, Government of India, New Delhi. Printed at Government of India Press, Faridabad, 1978.)

4

India have always been intimately connected with Indian religious life. The devout Hindu worships river water, bathes in it, is purified by drinking it, burns his dead on the riverbanks and scatters the ashes in the water. Temples are built along the edges and pilgrims foregather there. Fairs and festivals brighten the shores. So do the colorful garments which the dhobis (laundrymen) beat on the rocks and then spread on the ground to dry.

Below the plains are again mountains, the Vindhyas, rising only a few thousand feet, never in snow, furrowed with valleys and occasional lakes and covered with scraggy jungle brush. Tigers still roam in these woods. Frequently, on a summit, there stands a fortress with walls extending for miles down the slopes. To the west, across stretches of desert, the camel trains begin, while to the east, in a village in Assam, the average annual rainfall is 426 inches, the heaviest in the world.

The lower center of the Indian triangle holds the semiarid Deccan plateau. The steep hills going to the sea on each side are known as the Western and Eastern Ghats—a *ghat* is a bank or slope, and can also refer to wide steps by a river. More hills, with coffee, teak and other semitropical trees, and green rolling downs, lead to the coconut palm forests of Kerala, which shelter tidy thatched villages and quiet meandering waterways. At the tip are the breezy beaches of Cape Comorin.

Southern India has an even climate the year round. The coast and low lying regions are always warm, while in the hills, depending on altitude, it can be cool enough for a fire at night. In the north, on the other hand, the Himalayas have raw cold winters, with snow. The seasons are not unlike those of the northern United States. Because there are forests, the houses are built of wood, chalet style, sometimes three stories, with balconies and with roofs of stone, thatch and turf. In the springtime, purple and white iris grow on the roofs of houses in Kashmir, as well as in the fields. The mountain people live by farming, tending their sheep and goats, by trading and by handicrafts. Kashmir rugs, embroideries, silver filigree, and delicately painted papier-mâché are exceptionally fine. On the lakes at Srinagar, capital of Kashmir, are floating gardens, created from weeds growing in the lake, which boatmen, standing in long narrow boats called shikaras, wind up on poles like spaghetti. These garden islands really float until the roots of trees eventually anchor them to the lake bottom. In summer, one paddles by shikara through pink lotus blossoms.

The Ganges plains are dotted with villages, separated from each other by small irregular fields. In India, land has been handed down in families for many generations, to be divided and subdivided among the heirs. A farmer may find that he has inherited small patches of ground miles apart, which of course makes it inconvenient to till. Woodlands are rare, for these fertile areas were long ago deforested. The people in the villages live close together, in houses of brown clay or sunbaked brick, with courtyards and flat roofs, walled in from the narrow streets. Yet at

*On the backwaters in Kerala*

*Beach at Mahabalipuram, south of Madras. Temples are 8th century.*

night the plains seem deserted. Electric lights are scarce and the villagers go to bed early. All is dark.

The village day starts early too. The Indian farmer gets up before daybreak to bathe, to pray and then to go to his fields, with his plough and his bullocks. He takes his lunch with him in little

*Shikaras and floating gardens, Dal Lake in Kashmir*

*Rural India: one is never alone.*

brass bowls that fit one on top of the other, or has it brought to
him by one of his children. The littlest children play. The older
ones, when not in school, help their parents. Women do the housework and the cooking, look after the children (or the children
often look after each other), and gather by the well or tank* to
gossip while they fetch water. Village houses rarely have their

*Crushing the cane in Rajasthan*

own water. Their furnishings are simple—charpoys (light cots with
wooden frames and webbing) which can be easily set out at night
and stacked out of the way when not in use, a hammock for the
babies, a loom for weaving, beautifully polished brass jugs, cooking utensils blackened by smoke, and a faggot broom to keep the
house and courtyard clean. There is also usually a large chest with
locks in which to store the family treasures—wedding clothes, em-

* Artificial pools or reservoirs are called tanks in India.

*A village well*

*Water buffalo—and water*

broidered shawls, jewelry. It is not a lot by western standards—
but an Indian boy I met who had been to the United States told
me he felt that Americans are overburdened with *things*.

The best season in the plains is from October to May. In winter
it never snows; the days are sunny, the nights are cold. The warm
weather begins in March but the nights are still pleasant. By May
and June the temperature may reach 120 degrees Fahrenheit.
Sudden dust storms, though they cool the air, bring added dis-
comfort. In May schools close for the long holidays. The sun
shines down without mercy and people seek whatever shade they
can find. In the country there isn't much. The few who can afford
it take to the hills; everyone else swelters in lethargy. By then it
hardly ever grows cooler, even at night. Only the sleek water
buffalo, covered to his nose in his pond, looks comfortable.

As the temperature increases, so does the humidity, until finally,
about July, the rains come. When the monsoon pours down,
children rush into the streets and sometimes swim in them until
the water drains off. This is the time of rejoicing. The worst of the
heat is over. The barren countryside revives, the grass turns green,
crops ripen, birds sing, and the "Queen of the Night," a white
blossom like jasmine, perfumes the air. A favorite sport then is
swinging and ladies in saris, as well as children and men, can be
seen on swings under the trees, enjoying the freshness. Perhaps
some children rejoice less because, in July, school starts again.

The rains bring good harvests and prosperity or famine and
suffering, depending on how heavy they are. They can be too small
or too great. Huge dams are being built for water storage, power
and flood control. But they are not enough. Rivers can still wash
away fields and villages and make travel by road very difficult.
Where there is no irrigation and the rains fail, crops wither and
cattle die. Indians are still dependent on the climate which, it has
been said, has molded their character, making them fatalistic,
accepting fortune or misfortune with dignity.

In the early autumn of 1968, I was in the eastern Himalayas
when unexpected rains in five days washed away roads and

LEFT: *No water—even the goats have a hard time.* RIGHT: *Sikh boy, with topknot*

bridges, buried people and villages under huge avalanches of mud, trees and boulders, and flooded hundreds of miles of farmland. In contrast, the week before I had been in the west where it had not rained for seven years. As we were driving along the barren road to Jaisalmer, an old fortified town of golden stone, roughly one hundred miles from the Pakistan border, we saw a line of fifteen women in their deep red Rajasthani dress, moving slowly away from a well. They were pulling on a long rope. The rope had dropped a goatskin bag about the size of a laundry bag three hundred feet into the well, and as the line drew back it came up, one third full of cloudy water. One woman said they had no more vegetables in the village. The two bullocks which had been used to draw water had died, so the women had come to take their place. As they stood there, so straight and graceful, we wondered how they could survive and keep up their spirits on so little. They offered us tea. We heard that a canal was planned which could transform the desert into a green productive land, like the once barren Imperial Valley in Southern California. We wished it would hurry.

12

# 2
## The People
## and How They Live

It is as wrong to speak of the typical Indian as of the typical European or American. Indians are tall, short, thin, fat, fairskinned and dark, with faces round and pointed, lips thick and thin, noses sharp and broad, and all variations in between. Most Indians do have dark eyes and dark hair, which is naturally thick and wavy, though it looks straight when smoothed with coconut oil. Women traditionally keep their hair long, sometimes in a single braid that reaches below the waist, or wound into a bun, ornamented with tuberoses, marigolds or silver hairpins. A few now wear their hair short. Men's hair styles show even greater diversity—long, short, almost everything is seen, except possibly the crewcut. Some holy men shave their heads completely. Certain Hindus shave their heads but leave a long strand at the top. Tibetan men tie their hair in little braids. Sikhs never cut their hair or shave; they wear turbans and wrap their beards in nets. Sikh boys pile their hair into a topknot. Some Muslims like squarish, neatly trimmed beards.

Most Indians, when they meet or take leave, press the palms of their hands together and say, "Namaste." Some touch their foreheads with the fingers of one hand and say, "Salaam." Or else they shake hands—Hindu, Muslim and European elements are all part of the culture. India has been a melting pot for thousands of years as invaders have come, left their mark, been absorbed. Yet each

13

small region has kept its individuality. This applies to dress, food, customs and language. The Indian Constitution recognizes fifteen major languages, and there are more than two hundred others.

These languages don't even look alike. Here are three ways of writing the same sentence:

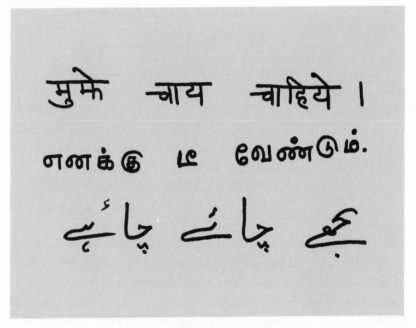

*Reading from top to bottom, examples of Hindi, Tamil and Urdu script meaning in English, "I want some tea."*

To be well educated, a child learns his local language, the national language Hindi, and English. Under British rule (eighteenth century to 1947), English had become the language of government and of the educated throughout the country, largely because of the good schools conducted in English which were established to train Indians for the civil service and the army. Rabindranath Tagore (1861-1941), modern India's greatest literary figure and a man of many talents, wrote poems and plays in English as well as in his native Bengali. Mahatma Gandhi, Prime Minister Nehru,

14

Mrs. Indira Gandhi and many other leaders of modern India attended English schools and universities. The constitution makers of independent India chose Hindi for the national language rather than English by only one vote. Some Indians feel this decision was unfortunate, since English has now become an international language. It is still used as one of the languages in government, in the universities and in the army because it is better understood by Indians from non-Hindi speaking areas and, for modern purposes, it has a far richer vocabulary.

Whereas Hindi is the national language, the language commonly spoken is Hindustani, a mixture of Hindi (based on Sanskrit) and Urdu (from Persian introduced by the Muslims). Hindustani has a double vocabulary, two very different words for the same thing. For instance, Urdu *kitab* and Hindi *pustak* (English transcriptions—from Arabic and Sanskrit roots) are both used to mean *book*. Hindi and Hindustani belong to the same group of languages, Indo-European, as most European languages do. At a school for girls in Calcutta, I watched a class of eleven-year-olds, in white blouses, blue skirts and long pigtails, bending over their notebooks. Their teacher said they were studying Sanskrit, "Like Latin, you know."

In ancient Indian poetry, to say that a girl "walks like an elephant" was a compliment. Elephants walk gracefully. So do Indian women. They wear their saris gracefully, too.

A sari is usually six yards of material, one end of which, pleated, is tucked into the top of a long petticoat. The rest is draped around the body and over one shoulder. The end piece can be brought over the head as a sign of respect or to shield the wearer from sun and dust. The sari is worn with a matching blouse. Saris come in a wonderful assortment of fabrics, designs and colors— silks, cottons, even nylons, plain, printed, tie-dyed, woven with gold or silver threads. There are fashions in saris just as in dresses. A sari needs no sewing, buttons or zippers, and fits any figure so that the variously sized women of a family can share the same wardrobe. Saris can also be arranged in many ways, even pulled

15

*Sari—Rama Mehta is wearing it.*

between the legs, dividing the pleats for freer movement. They are given as presents for festivals, weddings, the birth of a baby. A bride from a very wealthy family could have as many as four hundred saris in her trousseau.

Rajasthani women wear wide cotton skirts, four to sixteen yards around. They swirl them as they walk, always tall and straight, and often carrying loads on their heads. Women in the east of India wear a narrow wrap-around skirt called the lunghi. Girls from the Punjab dress in the salwar and kumeez, loose pants drawn in at the ankles and a long overblouse. Some Muslim women still wear a burqa, a white hooded cape which hides everything except their slippers and their dark eyes peering through mesh slits. In Kashmir, women have a long-sleeved, long loose jacket under which, in winter, they can carry pots of live coals for heat. In most of India in cool weather, men and women wrap themselves in large, woolen shawls. The most prized are those woven from the soft hair found on the neck of a mountain goat, so fine that, although two yards square, they can be drawn through a finger ring. Small boys and girls dress like their elders or wear shorts and shirts, skirts and dresses. The smallest sometimes wear nothing at all.

Indian women put on jewelry of all kinds: heavy silver necklaces, gold and enamel set with precious gems, beads, dangling earrings, nose rings, hair ornaments, anklets and lots of bangles,

*Rajasthani women—skirts, bangles, anklets*

*Lunghi—from Manipur, near Burma border*

*Kashmiri girl*

*Delhi on a cool morning. The black around eyes is both cosmetic and medicinal.*

*Kangra girls and jewelry*

of gold, silver, plastic or glass. When her husband dies, a widow smashes her glass bangles in grief and never wears any jewelry again. Jewelry is an investment, instead of money in the bank. Even poor families have heirloom pieces. In markets, gold, silver and precious gems are sold by weight and made into jewelry to order. Wealthy women have their own jewelers who come to the house.

Colored powders are used for makeup and for ceremonial occasions. Many women put spots of powder—the mark is called *tika*—on their foreheads. This custom probably originated with early Vedic (i.e., ancient Hindu) rites, when the priest put red powder on the bride's forehead as part of the marriage ceremony. Now unmarried girls also wear the tika, red or in colors to match their saris.

Pictures of princely courts show nobles in rich robes and turbans, heavily jeweled. A few years ago I watched a maharaja ascend his throne with so many rings on his fingers that a page walked beside him holding a cushion for a hand rest. But that was

19

*Tea country. Black umbrellas are carried, rain or shine.*

a ceremony out of the past. Modern clothes for men, except at weddings, are quite austere. A long tailored jacket is suitable for formal occasions. In hot climates, long loose shirts and pajama trousers are worn, or a dhoti—five yards of white cotton tied at the waist and draped loosely around the legs. On sunny days, men in dhotis walk from village to village under large, black umbrellas. Black umbrellas are carried, rain or shine. These also make little shops along the roads or shelter families of workers. The white homespun caps that one sees throughout the country belong to members of the Congress Party. They adopted them years ago, along with homespun clothes (*khadi*), as a symbol of independence from the British, who made profit from selling the Indians their mill-manufactured cloth.

In the Kulu Valley, in the Himalayas, shepherds wear short, white wool tunics with yards of black rope coiled round their waists with which to rescue sheep that fall into ravines. Higher still, in Ladakh, men wear long robes, fur boots, and tall brocaded hats with floppy fur-trimmed brims. In Kashmir, where most of the people are Muslims, men wear fez-shaped fur hats or embroidered skull caps. Holy men go about in saffron robes, or almost naked, their faces anointed with sandalwood paste. Rajasthani men like thick turbans of vibrant colors such as pink, red or orange; some are fifteen yards long. Naga tribesmen in the eastern

*Leh, in Ladakh, main street*

*Washing up in Rajasthan —note the thick turban.*

*Punjabi farmer*

*Outdoor life: a charpoy and a hooka*

hills have an elaborate headdress of peacock feathers. The vivid colors of Indian clothes stand out against the quiet browns and greens of the landscape.

Indians live outdoors much of the time. They often sleep on their roofs or in courtyards—or on sidewalks or beside the road. Most cooking is done outdoors in villages and in the poorer sections of the cities as well. The Indian stove, called a *chula*, is a three-sided fireplace of mud, in which wood or, more often, since wood is scarce, cow dung patties are burned. It is regularly re-plastered with fresh mud or a mixture of mud and cow dung.\* Over the chula may be kept boiling a potful of sweetened buffalo milk, so rich that it has to be diluted seven times with water. Indians drink buffalo, cow and goat milk. From the milk they

---

\* For religious reasons, Hindus do not kill cows for meat. Products of the living animal are valued, including cowdung, which is carefully collected, rolled into balls and flattened to dry on any sunny surface, often on the walls of houses. The patties are stored in stacks, like small haystacks. Cowdung burns with a heavy cigarry smoke. Since it is needed for fuel, or to mix with clay to make plaster for building, it does not go back into the soil as fertilizer.

make yoghurt, curds, ghee (a kind of butter) and very gooey sweets that Indian children love. For special feasts, a white curd cake is prepared, grainy like fudge, frosted with paper-thin silver, which is eaten, too. Thinly beaten gold was also once used in this way on sweets, by the very rich.

The staples of the Indian diet are rice and wheat flour, from which wheat cakes, called *chappatis* or *rotis*, are made. Maize, barley and millet are also ground into flour for rotis. In Indian cooking there are no loaves of bread; there is only the roti or else *nan*, a bread which does not rise. Most Indians eat with their fingers. Chappatis and rice rolled into soft balls replace forks for picking up the curries. It is proper to use only the right hand and to eat in such a way that only the fingertips are soiled. Hands are washed before and after eating. In traditional homes, the most formal meals are served on large round trays with many little stainless steel or silver bowls, each containing a delicacy, and everyone eats with the fingers. In villages I have seen banana leaves used as

*Ready for rotis*

*Grinding the meal for rotis*
  *"Dim dawn behind the tamarisks—the sky is saffron-yellow—*
*As the women in the village grind the corn...."*
                    *Rudyard Kipling,* CHRISTMAS IN INDIA

plates and glasses made of baked clay, to be thrown away after using, like paper cups.

What Indians eat depends, of course, on income, but also very much on religious belief and the habits of the particular social group, or caste, to which they belong. Some groups are more restrictive than others. Most South Indians, Hindus, Buddhists and Jains are vegetarians. Muslims are not. But Muslims will not eat pork and those Hindus who do eat meat will not eat beef. Some non-vegetarians eat only fish. Vegetarians have their own taboos. Some don't eat eggs or onions or garlic, some will eat vegetables that have been boiled but not fried, and I know of one vegetarian who ate only uncooked fruits and nuts when dining out. At party dinners there is usually a large buffet so that the guests may take what they want.

Indian curries are always prepared from fresh spices, and do not taste like the standard curry, made from the grocery store curry powder, that is familiar in the United States. Coriander, tumeric, mustard, garlic, onions, chilies, seeds of anise are ground into a paste and cooked in vegetable fat, to which meat is added or vegetables, such as potatoes, onions, cauliflower, eggplant, carrots, spinach, and kinds of marrow that Americans and Europeans don't have. Other dishes are made of *dal*, a brown pigeon pea that grows on bushes.

If they can afford it, most Indians have two big meals a day. The farmer's diet is simple—*roti* or rice, dal and vegetables. If he has cows, he can have curds, butter and milk, too. Poor families have vegetables or dal at one meal only; the other meal is just the roti or rice with salt, chilies and chutney. The very poorest try to subsist on the wheat or rice, and a little salt.

Many fruits and nuts grow in India, according to the local climate—apples, pears, apricots, almonds, peaches, oranges, limes, lemons, papayas, bananas, breadfruit, custard apples, mangos, cashews, coconuts and others not known abroad. Mangos are a delicacy of the hot season. They grow on big leafy trees and come in many sizes and flavors, from the plump orange mangos of Bombay to the tough-skinned mangos of the Punjab, which look like a small sweet potato but can be softened by squeezing and sucked like an orange through a hole at the top. In the south, the coconut is abundant and serves many purposes, in addition to its meat for food. If you are thirsty as you travel along a dusty road, a boy will shinny up a tall trunk to pick a green coconut. He hacks off the top with a machete so that you can drink the sweetish water inside. The leaves of coconut palms are woven into large mats for walls of houses. The fibrous shell makes ropes for fishermen's nets and doormats. Coconut oil is used for hair and skin lotions, in cooking and to light clay lamps. The coconut has also many ceremonial uses. For instance, before a play or recital the performing

*Good manners: always the right hand*

artists break a coconut on stage as an offering and for good luck.

India has long been famed for spices. Out in the country, patches of red and orange are chilies and peppers drying. Markets are bright with them, and with mounds of deep yellow tumeric

*Welcome to Kerala: coconut lamps and tuberoses*

*A market—chilies and spices*

powder, brown coriander, white rock sugar, nuts, cloves, cardamom, anise and green betel leaves. People buy little sacks of nuts and spices to eat as others might eat candy. Or they have a *pan* made up to order; lime paste, little pieces of betel nut, cardamom and other condiments are spread onto a wide betel leaf which is folded into a triangle, pinned together with a clove, and chewed whole. It is refreshing, like an after-dinner mint, but anyone who chews the betel nut constantly has stained red teeth.

Markets can be found everywhere in India. They are often in carts by the side of the road, lit at night with oil lamps. In the cities, there are many small shops under family management, rather than vast supermarkets and department stores. In the bazaars, narrow lanes are crowded with booths, in each of which a shopkeeper, assisted by relatives, sets forth his wares. Cloth merchants hang out silk, brocade and cotton saris, embroidered shawls and yard goods in bewildering variety. Gold and silversmiths weigh their metals on little balance scales they hold in their hands. Rows of booths sell tinsel, paper and glass ornaments for weddings and other festivals. Heaps of marigolds are strung into garlands in the flower stalls. Copper, brass, ivory, cheap plastic gadgets, precious gems, incense, firecrackers, ornate chess sets, inlaid marble boxes, everything imaginable—and things you can't imagine—are to be found.

In the wild animal section of the Calcutta market, my husband's bid for a large tiger called Mother Love was turned down. The shopkeeper offered him two hyena cubs instead. But, even at a bargain, they were not attractive.

# 3

# Delhi: New and Old

In India, as Prime Minister Nehru once wrote, the centuries co-exist. Ancient ways of doing things continue along with the most modern. While some cities now obtain their electric power from nuclear energy, most villages have only oil lamps for light. Jet planes cross the skies but, on the ground, people ride in horse-drawn carriages called tongas, in bicycle rickshaws, on bullock carts. Much work is done by animals rather than by motors. Bullocks pull ploughs and, in Delhi, they pull lawnmowers. You will see tractors too, and jolting trucks with painted wooden sides, but there are no large trailers. Heavy loads are still usually carried on bullock carts, some of which have been modernized by replacing the wooden cart wheels with automobile truck tires for an easier ride. In the south, elephants haul lumber from the forests. Oxen, camel, man and even woman power, as we have seen, is used to draw water from wells. At the same time, power plants and vast dams are being built—some by men and women digging basketsful of earth, chipping rocks, and carrying concrete for the walls on their heads up simple bamboo ramps. In India, people who need work are available at low cost where machines often are not.

The capital of India, Delhi, also blends past and present. New Delhi, where the government offices are, is a twentieth century city, planned, as Washington, D. C. was, to be a national capital. Begun in 1911, much was built in the next twenty-five years and much more building is constantly going on, pushing out into the countryside. Scavenging jackals no longer howl in city streets at

*Purana Qila, sixteenth-century city at Delhi. Recent excavations at this
site go back much further.*

night. Delhi also encompasses the sites of several earlier settlements. The first, it was formerly thought, was established about
400 A.D. and was attributed to a Punjab chieftain, King Dilleep,
from whom Delhi takes its name. But now new excavations in the
area are revealing objects from Harappa times, two thousand
years B.C. Entire monuments survive from as far back as the
twelfth century.

New Delhi, with its broad avenues lined with flowering trees
and its imposing red and golden sandstone buildings, is one of
the most beautiful capital cities in the world. It has many parks
which shelter old tombs and graceful ruins, and woodlands where
the wild green parrots flash through the branches. A great variety
of birds hover over Delhi gardens, waiting for an outdoor party
so that they can swoop down for a sandwich or at least clean up
the crumbs. The principal government buildings are separated by
a vast Mall, a mile of broad lawns, pools and fountains, at the foot

*Viceroy's Palace, now the Rashtrapati Bhavan, New Delhi*

*Pomp and Modern Circumstance—President's Bodyguard*

of which is a large stone arch. At the top is the Rashtrapati
Bhavan, the President's House, originally designed to be the residence of the British viceroy. Of rose sandstone, it is very grand, a
modern Versailles, with 348 rooms, a dining room table that seats
175, and requiring a staff of 2000 employees to run it. The extensive gardens behind the house are cared for by 500 gardeners.
New Delhi has pleasant houses and gardens, and also a fine zoo,
for which the high walls of an old city, called Purana Qila, are
the background. Further out are the mushrooming housing de-
velopments; downtown are shopping and commercial centers and
adjoining them is Old Delhi, until 1857 the capital of the last
Mughal emperors.

Before and after work in Washington, D.C., cars jam the roads.
In New Delhi, thousands of cyclists, long shirts flapping, force
honking cars, dusty little taxis and shiny limousines to weave
around them. Movement is further complicated by motor scooters,
often with a lady in a sari perched behind the male driver, three
wheeled taxi scooters, overloaded tongas, overfilled buses and
occasional wandering cows. Cows are undisturbed in traffic because, in Hindu tradition, they are sacred. But there are only a
few stray cows in New Delhi, since the government has moved
most of them to country pastures. Rarely now, the homeward-
bound office worker may pass a cowherd driving his humped cattle
or sleek buffalo through city streets, or a small boy prodding reluc-
tant goats. Along the walks, men squat, clipping grass by hand for
their animals; cobblers repair shoes; barbers give shaves and hair-
cuts; and a bicycle tire hanging from a tree means that a bicycle
repair man is beneath. Wayside peddlers wait beside their carts.

Old Delhi was once a walled town. Now it is entered through
gates left standing when parts of the wall were removed. The
huge red mosque with its marble domes and minarets, Chandni
Chauk,* the central avenue of Old Delhi, and the magnificent

---

* *Chand* is moon and *chauk* means crossroads, so this might be translated as
"Moonlit Square."

*Delhi Traffic I*

*Delhi Traffic II*

*Delhi Traffic III*

*Roadside barber*

Red Fort were built in the seventeenth century by the great Mughal emperor Shah Jahan, who also built the Taj Mahal in Agra. Around the mosque not long ago clustered booths and stalls where vendors sold sticky sweets, fish, meat (slaughtered while you wait), pots, cloth, rope, harnesses and old bicycle parts. Goats, cows, scrawny dogs and an occasional monkey rested on the steps below the entrance. In 1976 these shops were cleared away and relocated, but the people, rickshaws, carts, cycles and animals are still there in such numbers that you hardly notice.

Chandni Chauk, full of shops and alleyways leading into further labyrinths of fascinating bazaars, has dignified old mansions tucked away behind it. In Mughal times, a canal flowed through the street and on into the gardens, fountains and pavilions of the Red Fort. Inside those massive walls, the emperors lived with their harems, and held their public and private audiences in halls of beautifully carved and inlaid marble. Here Shah Jahan sat on his golden throne, called the Peacock Throne because of the two carved peacocks placed behind it, their outspread tail feathers colored by sapphires, rubies, emeralds, pearls, and other gems, beneath a silver ceiling at the corners of which he had inscribed the words:

> If on the Earth there's an Eden of Bliss,
> It is this, it is this, it is this.

ABOVE: *Jewelers on Chandni Chauk*

*Old Delhi roofs and a mosque*

Those days of splendor have long since gone, like the Peacock Throne itself, which was carried off to Persia in 1739 and broken up. Piles of jewels taken from it have been on display in the vaults of the Royal Bank in Teheran. Gone, too, are the courts of those rajas and maharajas who ruled the hundreds of states into which, even while under British control, the subcontinent was divided. Their powers have been relinquished to the Indian national government. From the walls of the Red Fort on August 15, 1947, the transfer of power from the British to the independent Republic of India was proclaimed. But any evening you can relive that history, told in Sound and Light, at the emperor's apartments in the Fort.

OPPOSITE: *Gate to the Red Fort, Old Delhi*

# 4
## Festivals

In India, festivals occur the year around. Regional or classical dances and music—singing, flutes, drums (especially the tabla, played with the fingers and the palm of the hand), the harmonium and stringed instruments, from the simplest to the intricate sitar —may be part of the celebration.* One summer day in New Delhi, hearing loud jangling and banging, I rushed out to see what was going on. This time, however, it was not a festival. Instead, the whole neighborhood was there with pots, spoons, any handy noise-maker, to scare off a sudden swarm of locusts.

Usually drums and pipes mean a procession. It may be a private celebration such as a wedding, or a religious festival. Since India, like the United States, is a secular state with no official religion, holidays of many religions are observed, including Easter and Christmas. I have seen Santa Claus arrive in a tonga and Wise Men leading real camels. Muslims have their special celebrations and, every Friday, services at the mosques. The twenty-seventh night of the month of Ramazan commemorates the moment that the Holy Koran was revealed from heaven. During that entire month all good Muslims fast until after sundown. On the last day of Ramazan, Id-ul-fitr, there are fairs and feasting. Muharram, an-

---

* Indian music is very different from western music in tone and rhythm. It is melody without harmony. There is no absolute pitch. The scale has seven notes. Indian music does not have a set form but depends on the ability of the musician to improvise. Percussion instruments are used almost constantly. Other instruments are the veena, sarangi, sarod and shehnai.

*Pipes and drums—in Mandu*

other Muslim festival, is a time of sadness; then big processions mourn the death of a grandson of Muhammad. But, since more than four-fifths of the people of India (83 per cent) are Hindus, most festivals you see in India concern Hindu gods and legends, and often coincide with the changing seasons.

Despite the many forms of their religion, Hindus believe that the universal spirit, the Supreme Being, is in essence one. Their gods represent the many aspects of this spirit. Hindus also believe that the soul goes through different incarnations and the gods, too, appear in several guises.

To many Hindus, the god Vishnu is the source of the universe. He has four arms, wears a holy jewel around his neck and a tuft of curly hair on his chest, and in his hands he holds the conch, the discus, and the mace and the lotus. He rides the great bird Garuda, an eagle with a parrotlike face. Vishnu is the Preserver. But one of his incarnations is another favorite god, Krishna, especially beloved because of stories of his naughty childhood and his love affairs with gopis (milkmaids). The loves of Krishna are the

37

*Muslim anniversary. The Head Priest speaks.*

subject of paintings, embroidered tapestries and poetry. Vishnu's consort is Lakshmi, the goddess of wealth and fortune. But she is also worshipped as Radha, the favorite love of Krishna, and as Sita, the faithful wife of Rama. Rama is the hero of the legend of the Ramayana, which almost every Indian child knows. It has also been said that the Buddha is the last historical incarnation of Vishnu.

To other Hindus, Siva is the high god, the god of fertility, of mystical stillness. For them, Vishnu is only another emanation of Siva. Siva is depicted as a yogi, in meditation, with his hair in a topknot. He rides the bull Nandi and his weapon is the trident. He has other forms, such as Nataraj, the graceful god of the dance. Siva also has a fearsome side: he is death and time, the Destroyer, wearing a garland of skulls and surrounded by demons. Siva's consort Parvati, the beautiful Mother Goddess, has her grim aspect, too, as the terrible Durga or Kali, the black goddess, who each year is carried on a palanquin to the river where she is immersed and floats away.

Brahma, the Creator, has as his consort Saraswati, patroness of art, music and letters. The kindly monkey god Hanuman, who in the Ramayana helped Rama to rescue Sita from the demons, is the guardian spirit of the villages. Ganesh, the cheerful, paunchy god with an elephant head, brings good luck. There are many others and many stories are told about each. Their images are found in temples and little shrines and in the *puja* corner of homes —to do puja is to pray. Gods are also honored by offerings of rice, by spreading rose petals before them, by anointing them with sandalwood paste, red powder and ghee, by dressing them and covering them with garlands. Religious observances do not have the routine and organization of Christian services and activities at church and Sunday school, but they are very deeply a part of

*Hanuman, the Monkey God*

*Manipuri dancers*

*Folk dancing in Mysore*

*Dawn in Benares*

everyday Hindu living. The devout Hindu bathes and prays every
morning, and goes to the temple or consults a priest at any time.
He may carry with him a little brass image of his favorite god
which he rubs as he prays.

Religion has over the centuries inspired most Hindu architecture, sculpture, painting, music and dance. Hindu tradition is very
old. Hymns, precepts and legends have been told by parents to
their children and by holy men, as we shall see, since before written history. The dance has long been, and is, a very popular way
of telling the Indian epics and other stories of the gods. In fact,
the words for dance and drama have the same origin. So, in India,
as well as portraying emotions, the dance is a means of telling a
story to music. The lyrics may be chanted with the dancing; the
dancer enacts them in time to the rhythm and sometimes sings
them him- (or her-) self. Some dance forms have been followed
for hundreds of years. Indian classical dances originated in the
Hindu temple.

*Puri—Juggernaut cars being readied*

The four main types of classical Indian dancing are the Bharata Natya, with stylized gestures, especially of the hands, face and eyes; Kathakali, from Kerala, in which the dancers wear elaborate costumes and masks or masklike makeup; the very graceful Manipuri dancing from the northeast; and Kathak, a more courtly version of the Hindu dances, developed in the late Muslim period. It was danced by courtesans, keeping the rhythm with anklets of bells, and is concerned more with sensuous themes, such as a lady's beauty. In addition, every region has its distinctive folk dances, colorful, energetic, expressing a particular mood or season—a battle, spring, the harvest.

The festival of Holi marks the beginning of summer. These rites are associated with sanctifying the fields for sowing so that they will be fertile, and to end the rule of a demoness called Holika. It is a day to wear old clothes because people celebrate by squirt-

42

ing colored water and throwing colored powder on each other. When you call on friends, you dab their faces with colors until they look like Easter eggs.

Every June or July, in the town of Puri on the east coast, the Juggernaut procession takes place. For months beforehand, huge wooden carts with wooden wheels are made ready. On these carts the images of the leading gods are taken from the main temple and pulled by hundreds of people down a very wide street to visit their relatives in temples at the other end. In olden times, and even not so long ago, frenzied worshippers would throw themselves under the wheels to be crushed to a holy death.

The god Krishna's birthday comes at the end of the summer—as with all Hindu festivals, the exact date depends on the position of the moon—and in Delhi, on many street corners, crèches are put up in his honor. They look like Christmas crèches except that the baby Krishna is always blue.

In Kerala, in south India, the harvest festival is called Onam. According to legend, this land was once governed by a great king, Mahabali, who brought such prosperity that the gods became jealous and banished him to the underworld. But because of his good deeds, he was granted one wish—to come back each year to visit his beloved subjects and to see them thriving and happy, bathed, in new clothes, feasting and making merry. It is a time of thanksgiving and family reunions. Before Onam, girls make floral designs with colored powders on the ground in front of their houses to welcome King Mahabali. Gorgeously caparisoned elephants and attendants waving fans of peacock feathers are part of long processions. Exciting boat races take place in the harbor of Ernakulum. As many as forty people paddle in one of these long, narrow, wooden boats with curved prows, called snake boats. Sometimes a boat begins to ship water. The eager boatmen keep on paddling desperately until the hull slowly sinks and all that is left above water is a long line of heads. On a river winding through coconut groves there is also a procession of enormous snake boats, one to two hundred feet long, with about as many people aboard, most paddling but some chanting boat songs to keep the paddlers in stroke. These do not race.

Autumn throughout India is a time of constant festivals. Dassera, meaning the ten nights during which Rama overcame the demon Ravana in the epic of the Ramayana, is celebrated for several weeks. Pageants retell stories from the Ramayana. On the final night, huge wooden effigies of the demons are burned, to the delight of vast audiences—and sometimes to the fright of those closest to the fires.

For Dassera in Mysore, the Maharaja held court, blessing everyone and everything, including elaborately decorated elephants, snow-white bullocks with scarlet and gold trappings, and even the palace cars, which were pushed into his presence since nothing must work when being blessed, not even motors.

In the Kulu Valley in the Himalayas, Dassera is a large village fair. The shepherds carry their gods, flat images of silver, from the hillsides to the fair grounds on a platform held up by hori-

*The Demon King Ravana—from elephant back (Dassera in Benares)*

*Well-dressed elephants—Dassera procession in Mysore.*

zontal poles which rest on their shoulders. At the fair, the gods are housed in tents and taken out to bow to each other. In the evening, the villagers stage wild dance competitions for which they have practiced for months. In Nepal, Dassera is still celebrated with animal sacrifices.

Diwali, festival of lights, ushers in the winter, the season of coolness and flowers. Little clay oil lamps are placed in the windows and along the roofs and terraces of houses, even in the lowliest hut. A window is left open so that the goddess Lakshmi can come in to receive her offering and to bring prosperity. It is the financial new year, when business firms close old accounts and start afresh. Children set off loud firecrackers. Some people play gambling games. Sweets are given, and presents. Wives and daughters receive new saris. The lights, the gifts, the holiday feeling are, again, a bit like Christmas.

# 5

# Family and Caste

In India, unlike America and Europe, parents, children, married sons and their children—uncles, aunts, grandchildren—often all live in the same house, sharing the work, the earnings, meals and care of the children. This is the joint family. The father is the head of the house and maintains authority, even after the sons are grown. Children accept this authority as a matter of course. The mother runs the household and she may also be a strong influence in the family, even if she is supposedly subordinate to her husband. Sons bring their brides to their homes. A daughter when she marries moves in with her husband's family, taking up her duties as a daughter of that house, although her bond with her own family continues. A festival called *Rakhi*, celebrated mainly in north India, reaffirms the link between her old and her new home. Each year, the girl ties a thread around her brother's wrist, meaning that she seeks his protection and support, if needed. He gives his sister a present, usually money or a sari, as pledge that he accepts the responsibility.*

Much more than in the West, a marriage in India is a marriage of families. Most marriages are arranged by parents who put much effort into finding suitable matches for their children, from fam-

---

* *Rakhi* nowadays is not limited to blood brothers and sisters. It has become an honorary relationship, like godparents, which a girl may offer to other male relatives or friends on whom she can count as a brother. It is popular with both Hindus and Muslims—girls in purdah do not have to show their faces to tie a thread around a boy's wrist.

ilies of similar background, beliefs and living standards. Formerly, and it still happens, the bride might not see her husband until the wedding. She sometimes wore a ring set with a mirror so that, although veiled, she could look down at her finger for the first glimpse of her husband's face. Nowadays, the bride may be consulted and she often knows her fiancé and his family beforehand. In rare instances, if she does not wish to marry the man her parents have chosen for her, she may avoid it by tying a rakhi on him, for by this act he becomes her brother and marriage is out of the question.

Arranged marriages, not being purely romantic, generally work out well. Young Indians expect to come to love one another during marriage and, since they have so much in common, this usually happens. The traditional Hindu wife devotes herself to her husband's comfort. She waits on him, doesn't eat until he has eaten, and walks behind him in the street. One day a year she has a holiday, when she does no housework. Instead, she visits, gambles at

*Groom arriving, Punjab*

cards or, now, in the cities, a wife who can afford it may spend the day at the movies. But she does not eat or drink even a sip of water from dawn until she has seen the moon at night, in order to assure her husband good health and fortune. At the end of her fast, the husband serves his wife her meal for the only time in the year. Until recently, divorce in India was almost unknown. Now it is becoming more common.

In India, some parents plan their children's marriages very early. Marriages once took place between small children, although the girl did not move to her husband's house until she was older. If the boy husband died, the little girl was classed as a widow, even when she had never left her home. Widows in Hindu society were considered bad luck. They did not remarry and led a very restricted life. Or, in the custom of *sati*, they threw themselves on their husbands' funeral pyres to be cremated with them. Perhaps death at that moment seemed preferable to the dreary life they would otherwise endure. Child marriages are no longer allowed. From October 1, 1978, the minimum legal age for all marriages in India, irrespective of religion, is eighteen for girls and twenty-one for boys.

Hindu weddings are elaborate when they can be afforded–and some times when they cannot. During the auspicious season for weddings, many houses in the cities are covered with colored lights, and bright shamianas (large tents) are set up in their gardens. The bridegroom in gold turban and tinsel garlands, accompanied by his friends and musicians, rides to the bride's house on a garlanded horse. A little boy, a young relative, rides with him on the horse; he's for luck. The men of the groom's family often wear turbans of one color. They are greeted at the bride's house by the men of her family, all with turbans of another color. If the bride lives far away, the well-to-do groom's family may hire one or several railway cars to transport the wedding party. On country roads, on the other hand, wooden carts with colorful canopies bring the bride and groom to their home with the groom's family after the ceremony. The poorest villager feels obliged to provide the best possible sendoff for his daughters.

*Wedding cart, on the road to Agra*

Hindu weddings used to go on for days, with much ceremony and feasting. Now they may last only a few hours. The bride usually wears a red sari, the end of which covers her head.* The moment of marriage occurs when the priest ties the end of the bride's sari to the scarf around the bridegroom's neck and, knotted together, the pair walk seven times around the ceremonial fire.

A Muslim marriage is always a contract signed by both parties, to which the priest (maulvi) gets the consent of each. Unlike the Hindu or Christian wedding, where the bride and groom take their vows together, the Muslim bride and groom stay in separate quarters, she with her women relatives and friends, he with the men, until after the formalities and the feasting are over. Some Muslim women observe purdah all their lives and do not appear in public with men.

A joint family has many advantages. Children always have

---

* Only the Indian Christian bride is married in white. If a Hindu bride wears white, her sari always has a colored border of yellow, orange, or red. Plain white saris are worn by widows, since in India white rather than black is the color of mourning.

*Ceremonial fire, wedding in Bengal*

other children to play with. Parents always have babysitters to look after small children. Work of the household is shared and so are the responsibilities. Although times can be very hard, what food and shelter there may be is for all. If one member of the family is out of work or sick, his wife and children have a place to live. The busy joint family offers security and warmth, which is sometimes missed by young couples today, if they move to a job in a factory or to a government or business position far from home. In the professional world, because of the joint family, or a modified version thereof, a young wife may have more freedom to follow a career than young wives in the West, since she can count on her relatives to look after her children while she works.

The joint family system has disadvantages too—especially if the members happen not to get along with one another. There is no privacy. No one has the chance to be alone. Being always part of a group implies restraints and dependency and tends to curb individual initiative. Under modern conditions, particularly in the cities, the extended joint family is breaking up. But Indian families still feel drawn by bonds of kinship, even when they no longer live under one roof.

Moreover, many ceremonies other than weddings bring Hindu relatives together. When a Hindu baby is forty days old, they come for the name-giving, which also means bringing presents. When a little boy is about three, they gather for his first hair cut; that includes perhaps two days of singing, sweets and gifts. The pandit is called in for all these occasions, and even to bless the moment that the baby is fed his first cereal. Another family reunion occurs to mark the first son's transition to manhood; then the pandit ties on the sacred thread (explained on page 52). And there are the sad gatherings for funerals. Hindus are always cremated. The eldest son lights the funeral pyre for his father. This usually takes place by a river, at grounds known as burning ghats. Cemeteries in India, generally either Muslim or Christian, are infrequent.

Another traditional feature of Hindu society, very different in theory from that of a democracy, has been the caste system. Some say class distinctions in India go back to the time when the fair-skinned Aryan invaders (see next chapter) suppressed the dark-skinned early inhabitants, the Dravidians. The Sanskrit word for caste, *varna*, means color. It is known that by the sixth century B.C., two thousand years before Columbus sailed to America, Hindus had divided into four groups, based on occupation. These groups, in order of prestige, were:

> Brahmans—priests and scholars
> Kshatriyas—warriors and rulers
> Vaisyas—tradesmen and farmers
> Sudras—menials

Priests and learned men outranked the princes and soldiers because they knew how to perform the rites that had to be observed to please the gods. This highest caste was entrusted with preserving traditional literature and scholarship.

Beneath all castes were the Untouchables, so-called because any contact with them, even touching their shadows, would be polluting. They lived apart, avoided by all others, and did the work considered unclean—killing animals, curing hides, emptying latrines. They were not allowed in Hindu temples, or even to draw water from the village well. Neither Untouchables nor Sudras could be initiated into religious life as symbolized by the sacred thread.* They could not take part in any worship in which the sacred texts, the *Vedas*, were recited. Although none of these practices had formal sanction, through usage they became as strong as law.

Over many, many years, the major castes divided into hundreds of sub-castes called *jatis*, groups of families who followed the same rules and rituals in personal matters. Especially important were the customs for eating together and for marriage. Rules governing castes and relations between castes became rigid and complex. Every Hindu was born into a caste and there was no way he could change it. He died in the caste into which he was born. A member of a caste knew exactly what he was permitted to do and what not. If he broke the rules, he was not only ostracized by his own community, but expected punishment in the life to come. Hindu religious texts state that it is the duty of the orthodox Hindu to abide by the rules of his caste. There was little mingling among the castes** and, of course, none with Untouchables.

---

* In the three upper castes, an initiation ceremony was performed for boys between the ages of eight and fourteen, when a thread was tied on, running diagonally from the left shoulder to the right side of the waist and back to the shoulder. This signified the beginning of a period of education for the boy in spiritual and religious matters, and also vocational training appropriate to his caste—the Kshatriya was taught archery, the Brahman scholarship, and so forth. Now this has all gone, but a certain bit of religious education still continues as a ceremonial. The lowest castes, being unskilled, did not have any period of training and did not put on the thread.

** Caste rules forbade intercaste marriages. If an individual stepped out of his caste, as in the case of intercaste marriage, then the rules and regulations of pollution and purity in his caste no longer applied to him. They were only for those who remained within the caste.

Since the Hindu family and caste determined a child's destiny from birth, notions of achievement, of success, of freedom of occupational choice as Americans understand them, did not apply. A boy did what his father did. A girl knew she would be married into a family similar to her own. Personal habits, diet, ways of worship, ideas, prejudices, and skills were learned from the parents and passed on to the children. In Agra I once watched an old man cutting jade and agate into leaves and flowers to be inlaid in marble. He used a wheel file he turned by hand and a saw like a violin bow with a single metal string. He said his sons were also making marble inlays and so had his father and grandfather—indeed, he may well have been descended from the marble workers who helped Shah Jahan build the Taj Mahal, perhaps even using the same methods.

The caste system, like the joint family, provided a form of social security. Other members of the same caste helped those in trouble.

*Marble workers in Agra. They are descended, quite possibly, from the marble workers who built the Taj Mahal.*

The system also provided education, by training children for their jobs or professions. Moreover, in the absence of universities, as we have seen, the Brahman caste was invaluable in preserving and passing on learning. While castes and subcastes split the people into many groups, these groups were so close knit in themselves that, although India was often invaded, foreign rulers could not wipe out Hindu community life.

During its long history, many efforts have been made to reform the caste system. In this century, Mahatma Gandhi led the campaign to protect the Untouchables, to allow them to enter temples and to become integrated with the other castes. He called them Harijans or Children of God. Today, caste distinctions are illegal. All Indians have equal rights. Discrimination against Untouchables is a penal offense. Special opportunities in educational institutions are held out for them and places are reserved for them in the government.

New conditions have also hastened change. Once people could

*Weavers, father and son*

live in exclusive communities, shut off from the rest of the world, but not any more. You cannot determine with whom your children will go to school or by whom you will sit on a bus or railway car, or near whom you will eat in a restaurant or work in an office or factory. You don't know whose shadow will touch you on a crowded sunny street. But habits of centuries do not disappear rapidly or completely and, in private family matters, caste may still be a consideration, more so in the villages than in the cities. It is also because the people in your own caste are the people you probably know best. They are your friends.

In India today the caste system sometimes has benefits in reverse. In a village just outside Delhi, I was told, the finest house is in the Untouchable section. It was built by an Untouchable who had gone into the taxi business and prospered. He also had dug himself an excellent well. Untouchables in neighboring huts used his water. The other villagers had to carry theirs from a well a half mile away.

# 6

# History:
# Earliest Days to 500 B.C.

## HARAPPA CULTURE (2500–1600 B.C.)

The first known traces of human life on the Indian subcontinent go back some two to four hundred thousand years, to paleolithic pebble tools found in large numbers in the north, especially in the valley of the Soan River, a tributary of the Indus. Other prehistoric tools have been discovered in the south, possibly contemporary with the Soan Culture. Paleolithic man was a hunter and usually lived in nomadic communities. Slowly, he learned to protect himself against nature, to build fires, to wear clothes, and to settle in agricultural villages. In India, these settlements date from the fourth millinium B.C. They were small and not in close contact one with another.

The world's earliest organized societies with a system of government covering a considerable area developed first in the valley of the Euphrates, then in the Nile and then in the Indus Valley, in the third millenium B.C. The Indus Valley civilization, extending some 950 miles north and south, is called the Harappa culture, after the modern name given to one of the two large towns so far discovered. The other is Mohenjo Daro. Both are at present in Pakistan. Sites of small towns and many villages have also been unearthed. Right now, archeologists in north India are making important finds of sculptures, seals, and bronze artifacts from this

*Harappa toys*

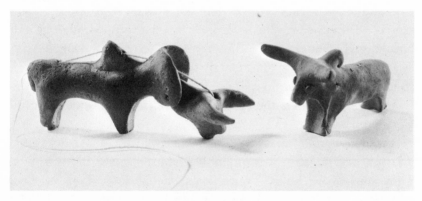

period, in Gujarat, in the Punjab and in Delhi. Recently, a man digging a foundation for his house in Chandigarh, in the Punjab, uncovered a goodly number of such objects.

From these excavations it appears that, four to five thousand years ago, the people of the Indus Valley lived as comfortably as many do today. They had houses of brick with paved floors, bathrooms, wells, covered sewers and cesspits. Many houses, quite large, of two or more stories built around a courtyard, must have belonged to the well-to-do. Workmen lived in rows of two-room cottages. A remarkable building, which is still to be seen at Mohenjo Daro, is the Great Bath, an oblong swimming pool thirty-nine by twenty-three feet and eight feet deep, of fine brickwork with good drainage. It was once surrounded by a cloister and small rooms.

Ornaments of gold, silver, and ivory, and beads show that the Harappa women loved jewelry, especially bangles, large necklaces and earrings. Their children played with terra cotta toys—little carts, cattle with heads that could move, monkeys that would slide down a string, birdshaped whistles.* Figurines and seals, which every important citizen probably carried to mark his own property or for luck, suggest how the Harappa people looked and lived. The men wore robes with one shoulder bare, beads and long hair. Women had elaborate coiffures or pigtails. One seal shows their skirts at just below the knee; a goddess is in a miniskirt. The pipal tree and some animals (bulls but not cows, for instance) were sacred. A mother goddess figure was worshipped and also a horned god, thought to be the prototype of the Hindu god Siva, as Lord of the Beasts (Pasupati). Other finds, including a black stone resembling the Siva linga, the symbol of Siva, support the theory that Sivaism is the most ancient faith still practiced in the world today.

Harappa farmers raised grain, wheat, barley, peas, sesamum, and cotton. The latter was probably first used in the Indus Valley. They kept cattle, buffalo, pigs, goats, sheep, dogs, donkeys, fowl and elephants. The usual beast of burden was the bullock. The Harappans were skilled potters as well as good masons and carpenters, and they carried on a flourishing trade with neighboring villages and countries.

---

* There is a good display of these objects at the National Museum in New Delhi and also in the Museum of Fine Arts in Boston, Massachusetts.

Some skeletal remains of these early town dwellers resemble the Mediterranean people of ancient Egypt and the Middle East, while others are the same type as the Australian aborigines and the wild tribes who, even now, inhabit remote hills of India. Whoever they were, they must have inhabited the Indus Valley for generations to have developed such a settled way of life. Their distant descendants are believed to survive in the present population of India, especially in the south, where their physical characteristics are found and where a form of Hinduism is practiced which has many features of the Harappa religion. A dance pose of a famous Harappan figure resembles the classic Bharata Natya dance of today.

## THE ARYANS: HYMNS AND LEGENDS (1600–500 B.C.)

The prosperous peaceful Harappa civilization disintegrated about 1600 B.C., because of invasions by tribes of Aryans who, coming from the west, first attacked outlying villages and then overran the cities. They triumphed because they had better weapons than the Harappans and used horses for their fierce swift raids. A semi-nomadic people, tall and relatively fair, inhabiting the steppelands that stretch from Poland to Central Asia, they lived a pastoral life, moving from place to place to find good grazing for their animals. When, as a result of expanding population or a shortage of pasture or both, they started to migrate westward in Europe, as well as south and east into India, they conquered the local populations, intermarried with them and introduced a way of life quite different from what had gone before. They adapted their language to the local languages of the conquered people, which explains why the Indo-European languages—Latin, Greek, German, Celtic, Iranian, Sanskrit—have common roots.

To the Indus Valley the Aryans brought their horses and chariots, and their tribal ways. Since they did not like to live in

*Konarak is a huge temple in the form of the chariot of the Sun God Surya (9th–13th century A.D.)*

cities, the well-built towns of Mohenjo Daro and Harappa were replaced by little villages that have long since disappeared. The Aryans also brought their form of nature worship in which the gods personified natural phenomena. There was Indra, god of thunder, Agni of fire, Surya the sun god, and there were many others. The gods were constantly warring for the victory of good over evil, but, although great and powerful, they sometimes showed human weaknesses. Priests chanted hymns in their praise. These hymns, passed on by word of mouth long before they were written down, are known as the *Rig Veda*, the most sacred of the many sacred texts of the Hindus. Composed probably between 1500 and 1000 B.C., Vedic hymns are recited at wedding, birth, and funeral ceremonies to this day and are familiar to millions of people, although perhaps not everyone understands them.

But it is hard to know what actually happened so long ago because, in the hymns, it is not possible to separate legend from fact. We know that the Aryan settlers who first came to the eastern Punjab (the region north and west of Delhi), eventually conquered all of northern India, which they called Aryavarta, land of the Aryans. As the ruling class, they suppressed the older culture, although the darkskinned inhabitants whom the Aryans called Dasas (slaves) and we call Dravidians, resisted stoutly. Ultimately, however, the two cultures merged. South India, protected by natural barriers, developed a distinct Dravidian culture but, here too, Aryan religion and ideas gradually penetrated. From the fusion of these cultures, Hinduism evolved.

During the next five hundred years, from the time of the *Rig Veda* to the birth of the Buddha, (1000-500 B.C., roughly, from the time of Homer through the early days of Rome), other hymns and legends tell us that the Aryans extended their conquests in the Ganges basin east and south to what is now Bengal. The two greatest epics of Indian literature, the *Ramayana* and the *Mahabharata,* originated then. They continue to be immensely important to all Hindus and are known to most peoples of southeast Asia.

The *Ramayana* is probably the older of the two and it is shorter. Although parts were added later, the main poem seems to have been the work of one poet, believed to be the sage Valmiki, a contemporary of Rama. Very briefly, the story is this: the venerable King Dasaratha, who ruled Kosala (its capital Ayodhya was near present day Benares), in order to keep his word to one of his wives, very reluctantly banishes his beloved elder son Rama to the forests for fourteen years. With Rama go his faithful bride Sita and one brother. During their exile, Sita is tricked and carried off to Ceylon by the demon king Ravana, but after many trials and a tremendous battle, she is finally rescued by Rama. Thus good triumphs over evil, and Rama and Sita are welcomed back

61

to rule their kingdom, since King Dasaratha meanwhile has died. Stories about Rama are told over and over and children are urged to pattern their lives on those of the heroes.

The *Mahabharata* is based on a great battle which may have taken place not far from Delhi about 1000 B.C., between the Kuru and the Pandava princes. It was not composed by a single author or in a single period. The core of the work is the *Bhagvad Gita*, "the Song of the Lord," the most popular religious poem in India. It is the discourse between Arjun, one of the five Pandavas, and Lord Krishna, on the eve of the battle, when Arjun asks the Lord, "Why should one fight?" The Pandavas and the Kurus are related to each other so that the battle ahead is a kind of civil war, pitting brother against brother, and will mean terrible bloodshed. But Lord Krishna overrules Arjun's objections, telling him that it is his duty to defend the right, even if it may appear that the immediate deed, the bloodshed of war, is wrong. The highest good is to uphold the right.

The hymns and epics, though partly legend, still give an idea of the Indians of long ago. The early Aryans were a bold, gay, unrestrained people, fond of drinking, music, dancing and gambling. Acrobats, dancers, flute players and fortunetellers were popular. Most of the Aryans lived by farming and tending livestock. Cattle were very important, for labor, for food and even as a substitute for money. The priest, the warrior, and the farmer expected payment or reward for their services with cattle. At that time cows were not yet considered sacred and were killed for food. Horses were also prized highly. India to this day enjoys truly skilled horsemanship.

The Aryan family was presided over by the father and continued through the male line. Women, though respected, were subordinate to men. Usually, a man had only one wife. The

*"Penance of Arjun"—a vast bas-relief, 96 feet long and 43 feet high, of animals, dwarfs, flying figures, humans, from the Mahabharata, carved in rock, at Mahabalipuram (7th century A.D.)*

tribes were ruled by chieftains called rajas (like the Latin *rex*), with courtiers and lesser chieftains in attendance. But the priests who performed sacrificial rites were of very great importance, for it was believed that the gods, if not properly worshipped, could bring destruction. As time went on, the small tribal groups of the Vedic age expanded into large kingdoms ruled by hereditary monarchs, although there was no single ruler over all India. The villages grew, too, so that, once more, there began to be towns and cities.

As princes and priests became more powerful, sacrificial rites to be performed became more complex. One which is often recounted in Indian stories is the horse sacrifice (asvamedha). A consecrated horse was set free to wander at will for a year. It was followed by a band of warriors. When it strayed into another king's territory, that king was obliged to fight. Otherwise, to allow the horse to pass through his land unchallenged and unmolested was a token of his homage to the ruler who had sent out the animal. If it was not captured, the horse was brought back to its home capital at the year's end and sacrificed. Every important king wanted to perform a horse sacrifice. But this was not a way to get along with one's neighbors.

By 500 B.C., Indian life and thought had taken on many features that have lasted into the twentieth century, even including kinds of entertainment—music, dancing and stories. New crafts and trades appeared. A wide variety of crops were cultivated and some irrigation was introduced. The basic forms of Hinduism were established. As we saw in an earlier chapter, society had already divided into classes depending on occupation—the caste system had begun.

# 7

# Hindu Reformation (500 B.C.):
# Buddhists, Jains

We have seen that priests were at the top of the Hindu caste
hierachy because they controlled the rituals necessary to appease
the gods. The early Hindus attached great importance in their
ceremonies to sacrifice, especially of animals. By the sixth century
B.C., these rites had become elaborate and very bloody; only the
Brahmans who performed them could understand their com-
plexities. The other castes could not function without the inter-
cession of the priests and were therefore at their mercy. With
power, the priests had become both arrogant and greedy, demand-
ing a high price for their services and threatening dire consequences to anyone who did not comply. On the other hand, at
the same time, a strict asceticism had developed, which also could
not have general appeal. Religion had lost its hold on the people.

As in Europe two thousand years later, a moral reformation was
in order. It was necessary to break with old superstitions, to
weaken the control of the corrupt Brahmans, and to bring religious
practices back in touch with human needs. The leaders of this
reform were two Kshatriyas of royal blood—Mahavir, founder
of the Jains, and Gautama, the Buddha. Their followers, although
they continued to revere Hindu gods, evolved new forms of
Hinduism, just as the Protestants did for Christianity when they
broke with the Catholic Church.

When Siddhartha Gautama was born, in a little kingdom in the

*Horsemanship today*

foothills of the Himalayas, it was foretold that, because of his concern for human misery, he would renounce the world and become a Universal Teacher. His father, the king, not wishing him to give up worldly enjoyments, tried to keep him in luxury, shielded from all knowledge of pain and sorrow. But Prince Siddhartha found out and was so shocked by the discovery that he stole away from the palace, abode of love and pleasure, leaving his beautiful young wife, his baby son and all his riches. Dressed as a hermit, begging his food, he set forth to find a remedy for human suffering.

First, he turned to the study of philosophy but did not find the answer. Then, for six years, living in the forest, he subjected himself to severe austerities but became convinced that they were useless. Finally, after he had sat under a pipal tree, motionless, in meditation, for forty-nine days, enlightenment came to him: now he knew why the world was full of unhappiness and what man had to do to overcome it. From then on, he was called the Buddha, the Enlightened One. Leaving the "Tree of Wisdom," he went to Sarnath near Benares where he preached his first sermon on the meaning of life. Stupas (burial mounds) and temples commemorate this site and sculptures tell the story.

Instead of depending on the rituals of priests, the Buddha taught that to find truth man must look inward. Sorrow comes through craving individual satisfaction. It can be stopped by no longer craving. This is done by living a moral and well-ordered life. The Buddha stressed inner discipline, purity of word, thought and deed, avoidance of luxuries, and respect for all life, including animal life. Animal sacrifice would not be permitted. The Buddha further undermined the power of the Brahmans by denying caste in every sense. According to his code of conduct, all men were equal toward one another and before the universal spirit. He was, in this respect, a modern democratic man.

The Buddha continued to teach, attracting many disciples, until he died in his eightieth year, between 486 and 473 B.C. His ashes were distributed to a number of places throughout India and buried in stupas. A beautiful stupa is on a hilltop at Sanchi, in central India; the sculptures there are more than two thousand

*Stupa at Sarnath, where Buddha preached his first sermon*

OPPOSITE: *Jain saint (Post-Gupta style, c. 700 A.D.)*

years old. Many monasteries were built. Sometimes the monks' cells were in caves carved from the cool rock, and are still to be seen.

Buddhists continued to be active in India until after they were overwhelmed by the Muslims in the eleventh century A.D., although their great period was over by the third century A.D. Buddhism still survives in the Himalayas, where it keeps its ties with Hinduism. In China, Japan, Burma and Ceylon, Buddhism has developed as a religion in its own right, quite separate from its Hindu origins.

Mahavir, who was related to the reigning kings of Magdha (now Bihar), renounced the world when he was thirty, spent twelve years in penance and meditation, and then became a religious reformer. He was called "Jina," the Conqueror, because he conquered human passions. From this came the name Jain. He preached in South Bihar, gathering around him many followers

*Ladakh, where Buddhism still survives*

who spread his teachings, and he died in Patna, which is between Benares and Calcutta, possibly in 467 B.C.

Hindus, Buddhists and Jains all believe in *karma*, the continuity of life through rebirth of the soul. A man's condition in this life depends on his actions in his past experience. The highest state of bliss through spiritual growth the Buddhists call Nirvana. Jains believe that a universal soul exists throughout nature, in inanimate as well as in living things. God is the highest manifestation of the good which is latent in the souls of men. The soul attains salvation through right faith, right knowledge and right action—these are the three jewels of Jainism.

Any cruel, selfish deed, especially any form of killing, prevents the soul's upward transmigration. So the first principle of Jainism is *ahimsa* or non-injury to any living creature. Jains would never eat meat. They dared not farm because they might destroy living things in the soil. Jain monks swept their path with feather dusters so that they would not accidentally step on an ant, and veiled their mouths so that they would not inadvertently inhale some tiny insect.

Jains were great builders of temples. Statues of their saints are not unlike the figure of the Buddha. Unlike Buddhism, however, Jainism has remained in India. Today, there are some two million Jains there, strict vegetarians, mostly well-to-do merchants. Jains stress honesty and frugality. They also look after animals of all kinds. In Old Delhi, there is a Jain hospital just for birds.

# 8

# The Mauryas (324-183 B.C.) and the Guptas (320-647 A.D.)

The sixth, fifth and fourth centuries B.C. were a period of disunity in India. Small and large states were constantly at war with one another and unable to meet threats from outside. From Persia, Cyrus (558-530 B.C.) extended his rule to the borders of India, and Darius (522-486 B.C.) conquered the Indus Valley to the deserts of Rajasthan. Coming from Greece, Alexander the Great (327-326 B.C.) crossed the high Hindukush in Afghanistan and fought his way into the Indus region, intending to annex these provinces to his vast empire. But his men, homesick and weary, rebelled, and he turned back—three years before his death, at thirty-three. Although his conquest was brief, through it Greeks and Indians were brought into contact with each other. Europe learned about India and India was exposed to Greek influence in art, thought and administration. Moreover, Alexander's invasion further weakened those states near the Indus Valley and may have encouraged a young prince, Chandra Gupta Maurya, to overthrow their rulers and to unify northern India.

The Maurya period was a bright one politically, artistically and culturally. Its sovereigns were able to mold the small kingdoms into a mighty empire under a system of administration still studied for its excellence. The people were well cared for and protected. In this atmosphere, the arts and religion could survive without disruption.

71

*Sanchi: The Great Stupa, begun in Asoka's time*

According to tradition, Chandra Gupta Maurya was a son of a Nanda king by a woman of the Sudra (fourth) caste, named Maura, from whom the dynasty took its name. Sent into exile, he was helped by a clever Brahman adviser, Chanakya, to overthrow the Nanda family. He ascended the throne in 324 B.C. When he finally also defeated the Greek garrisons left by Alexander, his empire reached from Afghanistan and the Punjab to the borders of Bengal and included most of the rest of India except the extreme south. He thus became the first Emperor of India.

Chandra Gupta divided his state into provinces under governors responsible for maintaining order, collecting revenue and keeping him informed. He set up a regular civil administration which, three hundred years before Christ, was a remarkable achievement. He also had a well-organized system of espionage so that he could prevent any one governor from becoming too important. These informers kept him in touch even with the most remote parts of his empire.

We know about Chandra Gupta's style of living through the account of a Greek writer sent as ambassador to his court. The royal palace, situated in a beautiful park with fountains and fish ponds, was made of timber and had goldcoated wooden pillars ornamented with designs of silver birds and gold vines. It was supplied with luxuries ordered from all parts of Asia. Many beautiful women were in attendance, to wait on the king. Hunting and animal fights were the principal amusements of the court. When the emperor appeared in public, it was either in a gold palanquin or on a bejeweled elephant. But his reign ended sadly. When a great famine occurred, he abdicated in favor of his son and committed suicide by slow starvation. This was in the year 300 B.C.

The greatest Maurya king was Chandra Gupta's grandson, Asoka (269–232 B.C.). We know about him through his own account, for in many parts of India there still exist rocks and pillars inscribed with his imperial edicts, pronouncements of his policy and instructions to his officials and subjects. These are the oldest surviving written documents in Indian history.

73

*Asoka Column,*
*Sarnath*

The young Asoka seemed at first merely pleasure-bent, like others of his age. But eight years after his coronation (261 B.C.), in order to expand his empire, he fought a war against Kalinga (now Orissa, on the east coast) so bloody that it made him heartsick. Thereafter, he resolved never again to engage in aggressive warfare, but to rule only through righteousness; he would devote the rest of his life to spreading the message of peace and good will among men and to relieving human misery. He became a Buddhist, adhering strictly to the principle of nonviolence, *ahimsa*, which, as we have noted, is noninjury to men and animals. He banned animal sacrifices, regulated the slaughter of animals for food and set an example by cutting down on the consumption of meat at the palace, encouraging vegetarianism. As the great patron of Buddhism, he appointed officers to teach its doctrines throughout India and sent missionaries outside the country to Ceylon, Syria, Egypt and Macedonia. Much Buddhist architecture still existing in India, including the great stupa at Sanchi, dates from his reign.

Asoka used his well-ordered administration to promote peace, but he also insisted on discipline—that offenders be punished and that every man should have the right to be heard and to defend himself. Special officers were assigned to prevent injustice and he himself was available day and night to hear complaints. To make sure that his instructions were followed, he appointed Officers of Righteousness, who were to encourage good relations and to check on local officials. Asoka looked upon his subjects as children and tried to bring them prosperity. He planted fruit trees along roads for shade and food, built rest houses and hospitals and dug wells. He believed that, through his example of enlightened government, he might persuade neighboring countries of the merit of his new policy and thus gain moral leadership of the civilized world. The new Republic of India has chosen for its state seal the four lions taken from the capital of an Asokan column at Sarnath, the Buddhist shrine near Benares.

However, by the time of his death at eighty, Asoka's authority

*Gandhara Buddha: shows Western influence in face and garment.*

was waning. Governors of provinces, usually of the royal family, asserted their independence. New invasions weakened the empire. The world was not ready for peace. The last Maurya king was deposed by one of his generals, a Hindu Brahman, about 183 B.C., and once more India divided into feudal states. The Asiatic Greeks, the Scythians, the Iranians, other Asiatic tribes came into the Indus Valley, the upper Ganges, Rajasthan and even the region around Bombay. Five hundred years passed before another powerful dynasty would give India a sense of being one country.

Still, those five hundred years were marked by artistic progress and by expanding Indian influence. Gandhara sculpture, for which Greco-Roman gods were models, is of this time. In the first century A.D., Buddhism spread to Central Asia and the Far East. Indian merchants traded by land and sea with Egypt and Rome, China and western Asia. Hindu kings ruled in Cambodia. The islands of Sumatra, Java and Bali were occupied. Indian art forms, legends and religion have become a permanent part of those cultures.

The Gupta dynasty, which lasted from the beginning of the fourth century to the middle of the seventh century A.D., is known as the Golden Age of ancient Indian culture. The Guptas were Hindus and, under them, Hinduism received fresh inspiration. The finest examples of Hindu art and architecture were created. Magnificent treasures of the sculpture and painting survive, such as the nineteen-foot-high Trimurti, or three-headed bust of Siva, in his aspects of Creator (Brahma), Destroyer (Rudra), Preserver (Vishnu), at the caves on Elephanta Island in Bombay Harbor. Buddhism also inspired artists who carved the caves of Ajanta and decorated the walls with wonderful paintings which tell stories of the Buddha, of princes and princesses, and depict the life of those times—the courts, the clothes, the markets, elephant processions, river bathing, dancers, and even one lovely

*Trimurti—three heads of Siva, "The Trimurti . . . might well be the many-faced statue of India herself," Jawaharlal Nehru,* DISCOVERY OF INDIA

lady putting on her lipstick. Hidden in the curved cliffs of a remote valley northwest of Bombay, these caves were forgotten for
ages, until in 1819 some British officers ran into one while chasing
a tiger.

At nearby Ellora are equally remarkable Hindu, Buddhist
and Jain rock temples and caves. From the end of the Gupta
period and continuing for several centuries, stonecutters dug temples out of the solid rock, starting from the top of the hill and
working down into it. Some of these temples are three stories deep
and decorated with sculptures which are part of the same rock.
To carve out the largest temple, the stonecutters had to remove
three million cubic feet of rock. This made a pit one hundred
seven feet deep. A huge stone block left in the center became
the temple, elaborately sculptured, rising from the bottom of what
had been the rocky hill.

The first Gupta, Chandra Gupta I (320–330 A.D.), ruled the

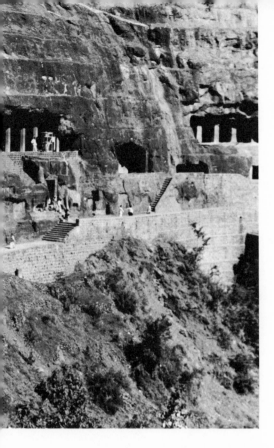

*Ajanta: these caves were
hidden for centuries.*

same region south of Nepal which had been Chandra Gupta
Maurya's capital. Eventually, the territory under Gupta influence
almost equaled that under Asoka, although it was never so tightly
organized. In the reign of Chandra Gupta II (375–413 A.D.), more
than 1100 years before the time of Shakespeare, India's greatest
poet and dramatist, Kalidasa, composed verses that are still admired for their delicate beauty. A Chinese Buddhist monk, Fa-
hsien, who came to India then, reported that he found a well-run
administration and a prosperous, contented people. Crime was
rare and capital punishment was not inflicted. Taxes were not
oppressive. Officials were not feared. He also noted that all re-
spectable people were vegetarians; only the lowest classes ate
meat. One could travel freely and safely throughout the country.
Passports were not needed. Foreign scholars were welcome and
were left in peace to pursue their studies. The land was rich and
its riches went to the people. Indeed, at that time, when the

Roman Empire was declining and China was in deep turmoil, India may have been the most civilized and the happiest country in the world.

But this was not to last. The Huns, those fierce tribes from Central Asia, spread devastation far and wide. One group, under Attila, ravaged Europe. Others swooped down on Persia and India in the fifth century A.D. Several attacks were repulsed by the Gupta kings, but each attack left the empire weaker until, finally, about 500 A.D., western India was in the power of Hun kings. However, they were soon defeated and those who remained in India were absorbed into Hindu society. It is believed that many of the Rajput clans, renowned for their fierce bravery, are descendants of the Huns.

In the first half of the seventh century, the Gupta empire was partly revived by a strong overlord, Harsha (606–647 A.D.), who was energetic, just, and devoted to philosophy and literature. He traveled constantly through his provinces to maintain control. But when he died without heirs, his empire disintegrated and India again was broken up by the rivalry of little kingdoms.

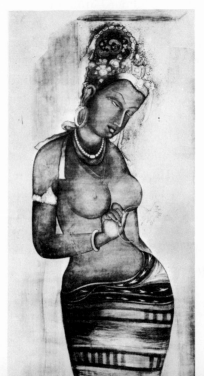

*Ajanta: wall painting of Yashodhara, wife of the Buddha*

OPPOSITE: *Ellora: temple cut from solid rock*

# 9

# The Muslim Conquest

Rock temples, tanks with their stone steps leading down to water, little shrines to Hindu gods along the wayside—all of these are familiar sights in India. But so are minarets and rounded domes. The latter were the work of the Muslims, who first appeared in Sind, now in Pakistan, in the eighth century, and who, from the twelfth to the eighteenth century, ruled large parts of India.

The Muslims were great builders. They introduced to India new materials, concrete and mortar, and new forms of architecture, notably the dome and the broken arch. Wherever they went —and they often shifted their capitals—they built vast forts and palaces, mosques and tombs, decorated with floral and geometric patterns and texts from the Koran. These we can still visit and see how the kings, their harems, and their courtiers once lived.

The Muslims not only changed the Indian landscape. They have deeply affected the life of the subcontinent ever since. Unlike earlier invaders, they were not absorbed by Hinduism. To this day, Muslim communities exist side by side with Hindu communities, each keeping to their own distinctive ways. Yet they are both part of India. Modern Indian culture is a synthesis of Hindu and Muslim cultures, a synthesis encouraged by the great Muslim rulers of the sixteenth and seventeenth centuries. The first Muslim conquerors treated the Hindus as inferiors, forcing them to pay a special tax known as Jizya and allowing them to hold only minor positions in the state. Many Hindus converted to Islam, but many others observed caste all the more rigidly. Some sultans were

*Elderly Rajputs, ancient fort*

cruel, some generous, and many both at once. They exercised their authority through a strong army. They could not have ruled without it because they did not have the loyalty of their Hindu subjects.

The Muslims met the most stubborn resistance from the Rajputs, who inhabited the hills and desert west of Delhi and were early rulers of Delhi itself. These warrior clans—perhaps, as has been noted, descended from the Huns—were the military aristocracy of the Hindus. Chivalrous and bold, they were quite the opposite of the gentle Asokan ideal. Each clan had its hereditary chieftain and was bound by ties of kinship. Fellow clansmen would die to maintain their own prestige but would not help a rival group. After the fall of Harsha's kingdom, independent states arose with no overlord to hold them together. So, though individ-

*Qutb Minar*

ually the Rajputs fought bravely, they were finally defeated by the common enemy.

The Muslims were disunited, too. Succession was often decided by bloody wars among heirs, by sons murdering their fathers and their brothers—the successor being the last survivor. Or, as the sultans acquired new territories, they would leave viceroys in command who might then become independent and set up their own line of rulers. But the Muslims were strong because of their faith. They believed in one God for whom Muhammad was the Last Prophet. They believed in the Koran, their Holy Book, and based their government on its precepts. And they strongly disapproved of the worship of idols. So they vandalized Hindu temples, destroying images of gods, animals and human figures. This also proved to be good economics. Sultan Mahmud Ghazni of Afghanistan, between 1001 and 1027 A.D., made seventeen raids into India, each time bringing back home with him caravans of slaves and gold, silver and jewels, much of which he had "righteously" removed from Hindu temples. At the temple of Somnath, on the shores of the Arabian Sea, it is said that Mahmud, although he was implored to spare the idol, cleft it asunder, and diamonds, rubies and pearls poured forth.

Mahmud Ghazni came to India for plunder and did not try to rule. One hundred and fifty years later, Muhammad Ghori (i.e., from Ghor, also in Afghanistan) rode south for conquest. A Rajput, Prithwi Raj, then ruled Delhi. He had become king by performing the horse sacrifice and was chosen in marriage by the beautiful princess Sunjucta. In 1191, Prithwi Raj drove Muhammad Ghori back, but the next year he was killed in battle against a much larger invading army. The princess in her bridal jewels mounted his funeral pyre to perish in the flames. Never, since that time, has a Rajput ruled in Delhi.

Muhammad put his favorite slave, Qutb-ud-din Aibak, in charge of his Delhi headquarters. When Muhammad was assassinated in 1206, Qutb-ud-din became the first sultan of Delhi, beginning the "Slave Dynasty" that lasted eighty-five years. Using stones from Prithwi Raj's fort and temples, Qutb-ud-din built a mosque and started a tower, the Qutb Minar, the tallest minaret in the world, which is now on the edge of New Delhi. The slave kings conquered northern India and fought off the fearsome Ghengis

*A Lodi tomb, New Delhi*

Khan. One of the kings wanted his daughter rather than his worthless sons to succeed him. She ruled well, but, alas, was deposed by her generals, who were averse to being governed by a woman.

Five miles from the Qutb Minar are the broken walls, seven miles around, of a huge citadel, Tughlaqabad, built in the fourteenth century by Tughlaq Shah, the first king of the Tughlaq dynasty. He was murdered by his son, Muhammad Tughlaq, a whimsical despot who taxed his subjects to beggary. Muhammad Tughlaq decided to move his capital a thousand miles south, to Daulatabad, in order to be more in the center of his country, and forced all the families of Delhi to go with him. On the way, many died. The Tughlaq tomb, of both father and son, across the road from the ruins of Tughlaqabad, is now frequented by amiable monkeys.

The next ruler, Firoz Shah Tughlaq, was loved by his people. He forbade torture, compensated those mutilated by the second Tughlaq, lightened taxation and did not persecute the Hindus. He built another city at Delhi called Firozabad. What is left of it is now a park. Firoz Shah was fond of hunting, and once lost himself so completely on an elephant hunt, so they say, that no word of him reached Delhi for nine months. His only fault reputedly was that he liked wine. Firoz Shah died at ninety and is buried at Hauz Khas, a series of pavilions and courts that once overlooked a large lake. Now people go there to stroll or read or picnic.

After Firoz Shah, there were no more good rulers of Delhi for a long time. In 1398, Timur the Lame (Tamerlane) came down from Central Asia. He looted the Punjab and sacked Delhi, collecting a tremendous booty and taking back with him thousands of artisans and masons to build in Samarkand, his capital, a mosque that would surpass all others in the world. The Afghan Lodi kings then supplanted Timur's men. Some of their blue-domed tombs are in a pretty park in New Delhi called Lodi Gardens. The Lodis left only their tombs. They were weak monarchs, and India again divided into petty, warring states.

# 10
## The Great Mughals

The sixteenth and seventeenth centuries were a time of adventure and artistic and intellectual achievement in many parts of the world—the Renaissance in Europe, the Elizabethan Age, Louis XIV and Versailles, the exploration of America. It was also one of the great periods in the history of India and the time when the Muslim and Hindu cultures most nearly merged. Six emperors ruled during these years.

*Babur (1526–1530)*

In 1526, on the plains of Panipat, fifty-five miles north of Delhi, a place of many battles, the last Lodi sultan was killed by invaders from Kabul in Afghanistan. They were led by Babur, who was then proclaimed king of Delhi. Although the Lodi army was three times larger, Babur had cannon which terrified the Lodis' elephants. Among his able generals was Humayun, his son by his favorite wife Maham, "The Moon." To celebrate this victory, Babur sent back eleven pence to everyone in Kabul and gifts of gems and cloth, which he chose himself, for all the royal harem.

Babur, born in 1483, came from a small kingdom in Central Asia and was descended both from the Mongol Ghengis Khan and from Timur the Lame. His dynasty in India is called Mughal, from Mongol. Strong and fearless, he was a bold and generous soldier who spent his early years riding and drinking with his followers. But he also loved nature, women and poetry, and sometimes composed verses as he galloped in pursuit of the enemy.

In 1527, Babur routed the Rajputs and went to live in Agra, down the river from Delhi. But he was homesick for Kabul and as yet no admirer of India. "Hindustan is a country that has no pleasures to recommend it," he wrote, "no good horses, no good fish, no grapes or muskmelons, no good fruits, no ice or cold water, no good food or bread, no baths or colleges, no candles, no torches, not even a candlestick." Later emperors remedied this by building marble palaces cooled by fountains and running water, with gardens, elegant baths inlaid with hundreds of little mirrors, and crystal chandeliers. They brought ice, packed in sawdust, by camel, mule and elephant, all the way from the Himalayas, a trip of two to three weeks. Babur himself laid out rose gardens and built marble pavilions but he did not have long to enjoy them. His beloved son, Humayun, was taken ill. To save the young man's life, a holy man told the king that he would have to give up the most precious thing he had. Babur knew that this was not, as his nobles supposed, the large Koh-i-Noor diamond, which is now among the British crown jewels in the Tower of London, but his own life. He went three times around his son's bed, fell ill and died. Humayun recovered. Babur is buried in a quiet garden in Kabul.

### Humayun (1530–1556)

Humayun at twenty-three was left an empire but he could not hold it. Although personally brave, his pastimes were drinking, poetry and opium. Forced into exile by a revolt led by an Afghan, Sher Shah, he spent fifteen years as a homeless refugee. In October 1542, after he had escaped across the Rajasthan desert, a son was born to him in Sind—Akbar, who would become the greatest of the Mughals. But Humayun had not the wherewithal to celebrate. With his few followers, he fled on to Persia while Akbar was entrusted to a great-aunt, Babur's sister, in Kabul.

Sher Shah meanwhile ruled Delhi, and wisely. He built there

*Humayun's Tomb*

88

yet another city, the Purana Qila (meaning Old Fort), which still survives. The Delhi Zoo, as we have seen, adjoins it. After Sher Shah's death, Humayun fought his way back and was once more recognized as king. Six months later, coming from his library in the Purana Qila, he stumbled over a parapet, fell down a staircase, and died. If there was a chance of stumbling, someone said, Humayun was not the man to miss it. However, his widow built for him, in Delhi, near the shore of the Jumna, the impressive tomb of red sandstone and white marble which became a model for the Taj Mahal. There he reposes, along with most of his descendants, those insufficiently distinguished to have tombs of their own. By moonlight Humayun's tomb is especially beautiful.

*Mandu, City of Joy—Sultan's Palace*

*Akbar (1556–1605)*

Akbar was thirteen when his father died. A wise guardian helped him establish control of his court. At eighteen he decided to be on his own. His first act was to extend and secure his empire until it included what is today northern and central India, and Pakistan and Afghanistan as well.

In 1567, Akbar sent his foster-brother Adham to subdue the kingdom of Malwa, south of Rajasthan, then ruled by Baz Bahadur, who lived at Mandu. Known as the "City of Joy," Mandu is now a vast, deserted ruin, but many romantic stories are connected with its past. Situated on a high plateau encircled by rocky cliffs, ravines and thirty-seven miles of gray stone walls, it contains marvelous palaces. One was for a sultan who chose to have only women, fifteen hundred of them, in his court. The palace of Baz Bahadur is on the top of the hill, with the pavilion looking out over the green valley where his talented Hindu mistress, Rupmati, sang to him of love. Their love is the theme of many paintings. Baz Bahadur was so enamored that he would not stir out to fight until Akbar's armies were twenty miles away. He was quickly beaten and his treasures, family, and harem fell to Adham, including Rupmati. But when Adham came to claim her, he found her dressed in fine robes, lying motionless on her couch. She had taken poison rather than submit. Baz Bahadur was more practical. He later accepted service under Akbar.

That same year, Akbar himself set out to quell the Rajputs. He finally took Chitor, a mighty fortress in the hills between Jaipur and Udaipur, eight miles long and three miles wide, with walls rising straight up from sheer rock cliffs. Rajput ballads tell of the heroism of Chitor's defenders. Twice before the fortress had been beseiged by Muslims. The first attack was by Ala-ud-din, one of the sultans who is buried at the Qutb in Delhi. He coveted for his harem the Rajput queen Padmani, said then to be the most beautiful woman in the world. Padmani held him off by a ruse, but in the end, as his siege succeeded, she and the other Rajput women, in bridal robes and singing, plunged into a huge fire.

When the last Rajput warrior had been killed, all Sultan Ala-ud-din found on entering the fort was smoke rising from the ashes. You can still visit Padmani's palace and see where these violent deeds reportedly took place. At the second siege, in 1535, it is said, although it is hard to imagine, that 13,000 women dashed into the flames while 32,000 men died in battle. The princes of Mewar defended Chitor for the last time against Akbar. After it fell, they settled in Udaipur and built beautiful white palaces along the banks and on the little islands of Pichola Lake. The Maharana of Udaipur, "the Sun of the Hindus," still lives there. He is the head of the oldest Rajput princely house.

Not long ago, while traveling in Rajasthan, we passed a caravan of unusually handsome bullock carts, with wheels of highly polished wood, studded with shining brass and silver. Inside, for bedding, were finely embroidered quilts. The owners, camping by the roadside with their families, were blacksmiths, heating their irons over charcoal fires. We were told that they belonged to a caste of blacksmiths whose ancestors, driven from Chitor five hundred years before, had vowed that none of their members would ever live in a house again until they could return to Chitor. It seems that Prime Minister Nehru became interested and decided to help them. He saw that housing in Chitor was provided and persuaded a number of these gypsies to move in. He escorted them to their new homes himself. But, the next day, or soon thereafter, they were gone—back to their wandering life.

After his victory at Chitor, Akbar then tried to bring harmony between Muslims and Hindus. He abolished the Jizya, the hated tax on non-Muslims, and the tax on Hindu pilgrims, and appointed Hindus to high positions at his court. He took four wives, two Muslim and two Hindu. One was a Hindu Rajput princess from Amber, near modern Jaipur. Enough remains of the Amber Palace to give a feeling of its former elegance. Besides, you can ride up to it on elephants, to the one-tune music of a ragged three piece band.

Although Akbar had not been a student and, indeed, could

*City Palace, Udaipur*

barely sign his name, he respected books and learned men and surrounded himself with scholars, musicians, painters, poets, philosophers and theologians. He thought a lot about religion. Far from being a fanatic, he did not believe that any one religion could be the only true faith. Every week, men of different beliefs were summoned to his court and philosophic discussions sometimes went on all night. To end religious quarrels, Akbar even tried to establish a Divine Religion that he thought all people would accept. His idea did not catch on. Yet under Akbar, no one was persecuted for his faith.

Akbar appreciated beauty in all forms of art. Hindu literature interested him, too. Under his patronage, artists painted a series of pictures to illustrate the epics of the Ramayana and the Mahabharata. Akbar was also a daring warrior and rode the wildest horses and elephants. He was fond of sport, especially night polo played in the dark with burning balls. But he was not self-indulgent. He was a hard worker and got up very early to supervise the running of his empire. He usually ate only one meal a day and often dressed simply in white muslin.

Akbar was a conscientious administrator. He personally dispensed justice, saw the records, and checked the accounts and

93

activities of his various departments. These included departments for elephants, for camels, for the kitchen, for silver, for
intelligence, for the army. His army, which was well-organized
and maintained, included 12,000 elephants and 8,000 horses. In
addition, 5,000 female elephants were required just to carry in the
fodder. Under Akbar, keeping defeated soldiers as slaves was
forbidden, as was child marriage and sati (the custom of the
widow burning on the pyre of her dead husband), unless the
widow wanted to do it.

Akbar wished for a son. On his way back from a campaign, he
visited a holy man in a small village near Agra. When, shortly
afterwards, at that place, a son was born to his Rajput wife, the
happy father decided to build a new capital there. The child,
named Salim after the saint and later to become the next emperor
Jahangir, was, of course, half Hindu.

The lovely red sandstone city of Fatehpur Sikri, completed in
1571 and occupied by Akbar until 1586, stands as it was when he
left it, nearly four hundred years ago, for no one has lived in it
since. Visitors come through tall gates to paved courtyards that
once saw royal processions and elephant fights. These begin in
front of the long hall where Akbar held public audience and
meted out justice—offenders were sometimes trampled to death
by elephants. Beyond are the balconies and platforms, set in pools,
on which musicians played; also the royal apartments, including
the royal bathtub, the apartment of the queens, the screened galleries for the ladies of the harem and their sheltered baths. The
buildings have strange imaginative shapes. The royal bedroom
used in hot weather was on the lowest level. It was really a sunken
rectangular tank, containing a large platform for the bed, so that
the emperor could sleep surrounded by cool water. In the winter-
time, he abandoned this air-conditioning for the terraces above.
In the small hall of private audience, the emperor sat one flight up
on the dais, placed on top of a single ornately carved central
column. Those he was receiving stayed in galleries along the wall
around him. The galleries are connected to the dais by four stone

*Rejoicing at the birth of Prince Salim, at Fatehpur Sikri, 1569*

bridges. Nearby is the Seat, covered with a stone umbrella, reserved for the court astrologer whom Akbar consulted daily, even to decide what color clothes he should wear. Worked into the paving stones in front of a girls' school is a cross, each arm of which is marked off into twenty-four squares, three across, eight long. The emperor sat in the center and played pachisi, a kind of chess, using slave girls as the pieces. The houses of Akbar's favorite ministers, the court where the merchants came with their caravans, the stables for one hundred and two horses and almost as many camels, and the quarters for the elephants still stand. On the opposite side of the city is the mosque, designed to accommodate 10,000 worshippers, and the marble tomb of the saint, whose descendants continue to be buried there.

Fatehpur Sikri looked out over an artificial lake, twenty miles around, long since dried up. The city was abandoned after fifteen

95

years, perhaps because of a water shortage. Perhaps also it was in sadness, for, towards the end of his life, Akbar's favorite companions had died or been killed, and his son Salim was implicated in some of the plots. Akbar died in Agra, at the Fort which he had built. His tomb is at Sikandra, just north of Agra, on the road to Delhi.

## Jahangir (1605–1627)

Prince Salim worried his father with his treachery and debauched conduct. Akbar was hardly a permissive parent. At Lahore, to which the court had moved after leaving Fatehpur Sikri, Salim fell in love with a young girl in his father's harem called Anarkali. But Anarkali made the mistake of letting Akbar see her smile when Prince Salim entered the harem. For this, she was bricked into a wall alive. Years later, after Akbar's death, Jahangir built a tomb for Anarkali, with the inscription: "Ah, if I could again see the face of my beloved, to the Day of Judgment I would give thanks to my Creator."

*Fatehpur Sikri—the strange, imaginative shapes*

*Akbar with falcon, c. 1600*

When he became emperor, Jahangir tried to continue Akbar's good rule. Because he wanted all his subjects, rich and poor, to receive justice, he kept a bell near his room which anyone appealing to the Emperor could ring, day or night. He was also a great patron of artists; some of the best Mughal painting was done at his court. But gradually he gave himself completely to the pleasures of wine, opium and the arts, while his favorite wife, Nur Jahan, "Light of the World," ran the government. Jahangir died on his way to Lahore and his tomb is there.

### Shah Jahan (1628–1658, died 1666)

"King of Kings, Monarch of the Universe, Emperor of Hindustan"—of all the great Mughals to be addressed thus, Shah Jahan lived the most lavishly. When he held audiences, he wore a robe

97

of gold, ropes of pearls around his neck and a diamond in his turban. On his birthday, he was weighed in gold and the gold (at least in principle) was distributed to his subjects.* Artists, musicians and poets were welcomed to his court.

Above all, Shah Jahan was a builder, with an inspired sense of proportional design, and he built with marble and with gold and silver and precious stones. (At this same time, Puritans were building log cabins in New England.) In Delhi, as we have seen, the imposing mosque and the Red Fort with the Peacock Throne were his. But to me the Fort in Agra, Akbar's fortress to which Shah Jahan added elegant apartments and an exquisite mosque, is the most interesting place one can visit to imagine how the Mughal royalty lived.

Behind the thick walls of the Fort, up the ramps where the paving stones are worn by elephants' feet, were rooms inlaid with mosaic and bits of colored and mirror glass, walls of latticed marble, running streams once perfumed with attar of roses or bright with fish, golden-domed pavilions, ladies' bedrooms with compartments in the wall for keeping jewels, the openings of which are so narrow that only a woman's slender hand could reach inside. There is a courtyard to which tradesmen once brought their wares so that the ladies could shop in private for their silks and ornaments. Sometimes the emperor himself joined in the haggling. Underground passageways lead down to the river and to cool apartments away from the summer heat. On a terrace is a marble seat where Shah Jahan could sit, his queens beside him, and cast for fish in the tank below or, on the other side, watch lion and tiger and wild elephant fights.

Some distance down the river magically rises the Taj Mahal, the marble tomb which Shah Jahan built for his favorite wife, Mumtaz Mahal, the "Elect of the Palace," whom he married in 1615. She died in 1629, giving birth to her fourteenth child. The

---

* Some of this money was earmarked for charitable and philanthropic works. Some also, no doubt, went to the courtiers, as a birthday bonus.

Taj took some twenty thousand workmen twenty-two years to build. Skilled craftsmen were brought from many parts of the world. But, like everything else, this cost a great deal of money, and although Shah Jahan was extremely rich, his wealth came from his subjects. It became harder and harder for the people to support his expenditures.

In 1658, when Shah Jahan seemed close to death, perhaps from an overdose of aphrodisiac, his sons began fighting for the succession. The third son, Aurangzeb, by ruse and murder, won out. He proclaimed himself emperor and, although providing every comfort for his father, (Shah Jahan was still too popular for him to dare do otherwise), he confined him in the Agra Fort. It is said that Shah Jahan died in the little octagonal pavilion above the river Jumna from which he could look to the Taj Mahal. Funds for building a separate tomb for him had run out, so his sarcophagus was placed to one side of Mumtaz Mahal's. It is the only thing that disturbs the symmetry of the Taj.

## Aurangzeb (1658–1707)

Aurangzeb came to power when he was forty, but he lived to be almost ninety. History does not make him an appealing figure. As he won his empire by bloodshed, so he had constantly to fight to maintain it. He fought other wars to enlarge it. These wars were expensive and the people were already overburdened with taxes to keep up the court. Aurangzeb enforced austerity. Artists, poets, historians were dismissed; drinking parties, music and dancing were banned. To set an example of simple living, the emperor earned money for his frugal wants by sewing skullcaps and writing Korans and selling them to his nobles. Whereas Shah Jahan used to ride forth openly, Aurangzeb was afraid of his people. He had good reason to be, for, unlike those wiser forebears, Aurangzeb, a strict Muslim, reimposed the Jizya tax on all non-Muslims. Moreover, he added extra taxes for Hindus and vandalized their temples, thus making enemies even of those Hindus who had cooperated with the earlier Mughals. The Rajputs gave him trouble, but the main resistance came from the Marathas of Maharashtra, the region east of Bombay.

Their leader, Shivaji, is remembered as a hero whose daring and courage every child in India admires. Born in a fortress near Poona, the year Shah Jahan became king, Shivaji was brought up by his mother, who told him of the ancient glories of India. With his friends, the shepherd boys of the hills, he raided the lands of a nearby sultan. Then he turned on the Mughals. Shivaji was an excellent soldier. With few men and inferior equipment, he stuck to guerrilla tactics. His fortresses are everywhere in the hills above Bombay. Aurangzeb called him a mountain rat, but could not trap him, or keep him from nibbling away at his empire. Once the emperor tricked him into coming to Agra and arrested him, but

*Taj Mahal*

the prisoner escaped. In 1674, Shivaji crowned himself king of his region. He governed as well as he fought, with strong support from his people. After his early death in 1680, the Marathas continued to harass the Mughals until they, too, had to yield to the British.

Another threat to the Mughal Empire came from the north,

from a strong religious group known as the Sikhs. This religion was founded by Guru Nanak, who lived at the time of Babur. Guru means Teacher and Sikh, Disciple. Nanak condemned the Hindu caste system and the worship of images. He taught that there is only one God before whom all men are the same and will be judged by their actions. Akbar, with his interest in all religions, gave the fifth Guru Arjan some land at Amritsar, near Lahore. The Guru built a tank and a temple which, redone in marble with goldleaf domes, is now the Golden Temple, the sacred shrine of the Sikhs.

At first the Sikhs concerned themselves only with religion. Then Guru Arjan was beheaded by Jahangir. The sixth Guru, Hargovind, spent twelve years in a Mughal prison, and Aurangzeb beheaded the ninth. Under the tenth Guru, Govind Singh, the Sikhs girded on their swords. They forbade the cutting of hair or beards, all took the last name of Singh, which means "Lion," and became an army of warrior saints who fought bloody battles to

*Agra Fort. From here Shah Jahan, imprisoned, could see the Taj.*

*Golden Temple, Amritsar*

defend their faith against the Mughals and, later, against the British. They are still a powerful force in India, and the source of many officers for the Indian army.

As he was dying, Aurangzeb is reported to have said, "I came a stranger to this world and a stranger I depart. I know nothing of myself, what I am or for what I was destined. . . . My breath is gone and has left not even hope behind it." There is no great tomb for Aurangzeb. His body was wrapped in canvas and placed in a simple grave. After him the empire crumbled. Succeeding emperors were mediocre men who left the affairs of state to unscrupulous ministers while they indulged themselves. The period between accession and assassination was often brief. The empire was much weakened in 1739 when Nadir Shah from Persia sacked Delhi, carrying off vast treasure. Mughal kings lived in Delhi until the mutiny against the British in 1857. Then the last king, Bahadur Shah, a gentle poet, was taken from his hiding place in the tomb of his ancestor, Humayun, and exiled.

# 11

## The Europeans; the British

Temples and mosques, garlands, cooking smoke, incense, the rhythm of music—many things are strange to a Westerner first coming to India. But much is familiar, too. Afternoon tea is a custom, as in England and so, among the well-to-do, are soup-fish-meat-pudding meals as an alternative to Indian cooking. Indian army officers have the manners of men trained at Sandhurst (the British West Point)—and until recently, some were. Most important, the courts, the civil service, and parliamentary government are the legacy of the British to Hindu-Muslim society, as they also are to the United States. Those traditions became established gradually over the last three hundred years.

Like other Europeans, the British (from the end of the sixteenth century) came to India as travelers and traders. Trade between India and Europe was nothing new. It had been particularly active in the first three centuries of the Christian era and, despite Arab and Turkish conquests, continued through the Middle Ages, both overland and by sea from the Mediterranean, notably from Venice and Genoa. Encouraged by tales of India's wealth, those countries with no Mediterranean ports began to look for a non-Mediterranean route that, for them, would be cheaper. As we know, Vasco da Gama found it when he sailed around Africa in three small ships and landed on India's southwest coast, at Calicut, in 1498.

With this new route, India was increasingly involved with the Western world. Trading posts became settlements which grew

*Portrait of a European, late sixteenth century.*

into colonies, the last of which were taken over by the Indian government while John F. Kennedy was President of the United States. During the sixteenth century, the Portuguese controlled Indian sea-borne foreign trade. In 1598, the Dutch sent five expeditions to trade with the East, but soon shifted their interests to the Malayan archipelago, the Dutch East Indies. The French came, too, and remained in Pondicherry, south of Madras, for 250 years. Evidence of Portuguese, Dutch and French occupation still exists in parts of India. But British influence is everywhere, since it was the British who pushed back their rivals and extended their authority over local Indian rulers until, in 1858, practically the entire Indian subcontinent became officially part of the British Empire.

During the reign of Queen Elizabeth I, English travelers visited Fatehpur Sikri and were amazed that Akbar's city was grander than their London. In 1600, Queen Elizabeth granted the East

India Company a charter to trade with the East. After Akbar's death, English emissaries brought lavish gifts to Jahangir, and fascinated his courtiers with their strange clothes and manners. One of them became the emperor's drinking companion. Another cured his sick daughter. In return, Jahangir allowed the English to build warehouses for the spices, cloth and indigo they were buying in India and the goods they brought to sell. Little by little, by negotiation and small payments to local rulers, they acquired trading posts along the coast. Forts were built around these settlements and soldiers were brought out to defend them. Many of these soldiers died in their teens and early twenties, usually from disease, as stones in English graveyards in India tell.

The English were shrewd businessmen, and trade with India flourished. In 1690, at the mouth of the Hooghly River in the Ganges delta, the East India Company built Fort William. In 1756, during a local uprising, the Indians seized the Fort and, on a hot June night, one hundred and forty-six English men, women and children were pressed into a room eighteen by fourteen feet, with only two small windows. Twenty-three came out alive. The Indian *nawab* (Muslim ruler) blamed for the uprising was killed fighting British troops and the British gained control of Bengal. The site of the Black Hole of Calcutta is now in a bank not far from Government House, formerly the residence of the British governors while Calcutta was their capital.* For, as the East India Company expanded its territorial power, the British Parliament decided to send out Governor Generals to supervise its activities.

The English extended their authority through successful campaigns against other European powers on the one hand, and, on the other, by taking advantage of the internal dissension and conflicting interests of the rival Indian states, which the Mughal emperors no longer controlled. In the eighteenth century, the British were vying with the French in many parts of the world.

---

* It is now the official residence of the Governor of Bengal.

*Tipu's Tiger—European being mauled. Organ inside the tiger emits roars and cries of victim. Made especially for Tipu Sultan.*

The struggle between Dupleix and Clive in India was the counterpart of that between Montcalm and Wolfe in Canada. The British won in both conflicts. When the French were forced out of Madras, they supported a local ruler, Tipu Sultan, whose father, Hyder Ali, had bravely tried to drive all foreign powers from southern India. But Tipu Sultan died in battle in 1799 and, after that, the British took over most of the south. The ruins of Tipu Sultan's fort and summer palace are still to be seen not far from Mysore.

The British Governor Generals were able administrators and, with remarkably small staffs, aided by Indians they trained, they succeeded in establishing orderly and effective government. Courts were set up to enforce a uniform system of justice and to prosecute dishonest tax collectors—although the British reserved for themselves the right to be tried in special courts. Highways were guarded against robbers, particularly against a caste of Thugs who, disguising themselves as ordinary travelers, would

107

*Maharaja's Palace, Bikaner*

*Sitting room in the palace*

befriend their victims, then, perhaps, after a convivial meal together along the road, would quietly strangle them with yellow scarves, bury them and disappear into the countryside with their loot. English scholars began to study Sanskrit and ancient Indian literature and the interest of Indian scholars in these matters was revived.

There were also flaws. Warren Hastings, the first Governor General, was tried in England for self-enrichment by questionable means, although he was ultimately found not guilty. Lord Cornwallis, who was posted to India after he had surrendered to the Americans at Yorktown, in 1789 introduced a system of land tenure, known as "the permanent settlement," which lasted until after 1947. When the Great Mughals were in power, all property theoretically belonged to the emperor. To collect taxes from the farmers he appointed *zamindars*, allowing them to keep for themselves a portion of the revenue they collected. The British confirmed the zamindars in this right by establishing them as legal landowners, who would pay a specified sum to the government but could then charge their tenants whatever rent they wished. The zamindars thus became a hereditary landlord class. They, naturally, supported the British, but were not loved by the local people. Indian craftsmen and weavers suffered because the British imported cheap mill cloth and other machine-made articles in competition with their handmade goods.

Nor were Indians content with minor positions in the administration, while the British kept the important posts for themselves. Indian princes who had been encouraged to seek British protection against their rivals were not always happy to discover that, once under this protection, they were also under British control. Sometimes the English were very harsh to Indian ruling families. Moreover, they did not always understand Indian customs. The Indians, for their part, looked on the English almost as a special caste, and not always so high a caste as the latter considered themselves.

The last great challenge to British rule in India was the Mutiny of 1857. Had it succeeded, it has been suggested, this would instead have been known as a war of independence, for, given the friction and unrest, the rebellion which broke out in several parts of India was a real threat to the foreign rulers. It failed for lack of united leadership.

To maintain their authority, the British made extensive use of Indian troops. The Indian common soldier was called a sepoy. The fighting started at Meerut, an army post near Delhi, where the sepoys revolted because the British were believed to be issuing cartridges greased with lard and tallow, the fat of pigs and cows, commodities which offended Muslims and Hindus equally. The sepoys fired on the British and then galloped to Delhi, where they occupied the Red Fort and grandly proclaimed old Bahadur Shah, who had been quietly maintaining his small court on a pension from the East India Company, once again Emperor of Hindustan.

A month later, however, the British returned in force, blasted their way into Old Delhi and, after six days, retook the city. Some of its remaining walls and gates still have those bullet marks. British soldiers quartered in Shah Jahan's marble palaces further damaged them. Bahadur Shah, as we have seen, was exiled. Both of his sons were shot.

The rebellion was especially fierce in Lucknow, where the British were under heavy siege. In Jhansi, near Gwalior, the beautiful young rani (queen), like Joan of Arc, donned men's clothing and fought with her soldiers. She died in combat. She was twenty-three years old.

Eventually, British power prevailed. On November 1, 1858, Queen Victoria proclaimed India subject to the Crown. Viceroys rather than Governor Generals now headed the government. Indian princes who had remained loyal during the revolt received special privileges. For close to another century, British rule was secure.

110

# 12

## Reawakening

In the nineteenth century, a new mood came over India. As had happened so many times in the past, Hindu society was challenged by alien ways. Some Indians now began to feel that, in contrast to the humane teachings of the Christians, Hinduism itself had become backward and needed reform.

The first to be so concerned was a Bengali of an orthodox Hindu family, Raja Ram Mohan Roy (1772–1833). Brought up in the traditional way, married while a child, he was a bright student and learned Persian, Sanskrit, Arabic and English. Reading the Vedas, the Koran and the Bible persuaded him that all religions taught the same truth. The turning point of his life came when he had to watch a sister whom he loved commit *sati*—burning alive on the funeral pyre with her husband's corpse. After that he devoted his life to attacking such evils. He started the Brahmo Samaj, a new form of Hinduism, to which any Hindu could belong, regardless of caste, if he would give up the worship of images. It condemned the caste system, animal sacrifice and the worship of idols, and allowed widows to remarry. Largely through his efforts, *sati* was again made illegal. In those days, orthodox Hindus would not travel abroad because they would lose caste if they crossed the sea to mix and eat with strangers. Raja Ram Mohan Roy broke with this tradition, too, and went to England to urge the British to give the Indians better positions in their government. He died there.

Other reformers followed. They sought to rid Hinduism of its superstitions and to make it a force to improve the lot of the people. Some taught that the greatest service of religion was to help the poor. The inequalities of caste were condemned. Old restrictions broke down. Until then, you had to be born a Hindu to be one. Now, with the example of Christian missionaries making converts to Christianity, Hinduism also began to accept converts. The constructive revival of Hinduism gave Indians a new sense of pride in their past. So did the study of Indian history and literature, now undertaken by Indian scholars, and a new interest in architecture and archaeology. Under the direction of Lord Curzon and the later British viceroys, historic sites were preserved and restored, for which the whole world can be glad. This is one of the reasons that there is so much to be seen by visitors to India.

British rule also brought Indians from all parts of the country closer together. Communication was made easy through a coordinated postal and telegraph system, better roads, and a network of railways that are very useful to this day for getting around India. Recruits from many districts served together in the army. Common problems of a country under a central administration were discussed in a common language, which was English.

Even before the Mutiny, the British had started schools to train Indians for minor administrative jobs. Afterward, English education made rapid progress, especially in Bengal. In 1858, universities opened in Calcutta, Madras and Bombay. A few leading families sent their children to universities in Europe. These educated young Indians, who studied about Western liberalism and political freedom, began to wonder about the role of their British masters in India. Why shouldn't Indians have more of a voice in their own affairs? Why should the British have clubs from which Indians were excluded and refuse to be tried in courts with Indian judges? Was Indian trade unduly to the advantage of England?

Surendranath Banerjea (1848–1925), another Bengali, took the lead in expressing this growing national resentment. The government of India was run by a small, carefully selected group of men who belonged to the Indian Civil Service (ICS). Entrance was

Vice-regal outing. BELOW: Viceroy's transport

by open competitive examination and attracted some of the ablest men in Britain—the ICS was originally all-British.* Until after World War I, this examination was held only in England, so Banerjea went there in order to be one of the first Indians to try it. He succeeded in passing and was admitted to the Service, but because the British knew and did not like his nationalist views, they soon dismissed him for a minor irregularity. Banerjea, however, would not be silenced. He was a fiery orator and aroused his audiences to the discrimination practiced by the British. To discuss political matters, he organized in 1883 the Indian National Conference, the first all-India political organization. Made aware of the fervor with which Indians were voicing their feelings, the viceroy, Lord Dufferin, was persuaded to encourage the formation of a responsible organization that would keep the government informed of Indian public opinion. With the blessings of the British, on December 6, 1885, the Indian National Congress came into being. One of its chief founders was an Englishman, Allan Octavian Hume, who had retired from the Indian Civil Service in order to help the Indians redress their grievances. Banerjea presided over several of the sessions. In 1921, four years before his death, he was knighted.

The Congress at first was strongly pro-British and had high hopes of working out reforms with the government. However, when the changes they sought were not forthcoming, Indian nationalists grew more determined and the British, in turn, took

---

* It is quite remarkable that the British managed to govern India with so few Europeans in their civil service. In 1842, the total strength of the East India Company's Service in India was 776, all British. In 1859, the Indian Civil Service consisted of 846 Europeans. By 1879, there were 907 Europeans and seven Indians. After 1917, however, a new policy of recruiting half British and half Indians began. By 1939, at its peak, the number in the ICS had risen to 1299, 759 Europeans and 540 Indians, to administer a nation with a population then of about 350 million. (These figures are from Philip Woodruff, THE MEN WHO RULED INDIA. *The Guardians*, London, Jonathan Cape, 1954.) The first Indian ever to enter the ICS was the brother of Rabindranath Tagore.

*Bombay: Gateway of India and Taj Mahal Hotel. The Gateway was built to commemorate the arrival of King George V and Queen Mary in 1911.*

measures to suppress them. The first notable Indian to demand freedom from the British was a scholar and teacher from Poona, near Bombay, Balgangadhar Tilak, who organized huge festivals at which he gave stirring speeches. For this he was imprisoned many times, including six years of solitary confinement in Burma. In the next half century, many others—men and women—went to prison for their political activities.

In 1903, Lord Curzon decided to split the province of Bengal into two parts to make it easier to administer. This turned out to be a mistake politically—most Bengalis did not want it, and, in protest, Indian nationalists organized anti-British rallies, boycotted British goods, picketed shops and set bonfires all over the country. Imprisonment, exile, insults—nothing stopped them. Then in 1909, for the first time, the British recognized the principle of election and enlarged the central and provincial legislatures. But they also made special provisions for Muslim voters which did not apply to other minorities, thereby setting a precedent for a widening rift between the Muslims and the Hindu majority.

In December 1911, George V and Queen Mary paid a ceremonial visit to India. At this time, the partition of Bengal was finally revoked, as the nationalists had demanded, and the capital of India was moved back once more to Delhi from Calcutta. It was then that plans for the beautiful city of New Delhi were drawn up.

115

The Indians supported England in World War I because they expected to be given greater freedom afterward. When these expectations were disappointed, agitation for Home Rule grew more defiant and repression more severe. Meetings and processions were broken up by the police. Many Indians were arrested and some were hurt. In 1919, at Jallianwala Bagh (Gardens) in Amritsar, where thousands of unarmed people had gathered for a public meeting, General Dyer ordered his soldiers to fire on the crowd. The exits were blocked so that there was no escape. Several hundred Indians died and many others were wounded. Elsewhere in Amritsar, British officers ordered all Indians on a certain street to crawl on their bellies. The news of these brutalities, like Paul Revere's ride, roused the whole country.

In the crisis that followed, a new leader with a new program emerged. Through noncooperation with the British government and political action based on nonviolence. Mohandas Karamchand Gandhi in the next quarter century won freedom for the people of India. He was known as the Mahatma, which means "the Great Soul."

You may have seen pictures of Gandhi which show this little man dressed only in a piece of cotton cloth and sandals, holding a walking stick or sitting by a spinning wheel. Gandhi chose to live simply, sharing the life of the poor. He wore just the dhoti because that was all the clothing that most Indians could afford.

Gandhi was not born poor. His father was the diwan (chief executive) of an Indian state. He sent his son to England to study law. Gandhi then went to South Africa on a case, but when he saw the terrible injustices being done to dark-skinned people by the European settlers, he stayed for twenty years to defend them and to try to improve their lot. While there, he developed a new method of opposition, which he called *satyagraha*, or insistence on truth. Violence could not and should not be met by violence, but by passive resistance. If a law was wrong, you should disobey it, even though you would have to take the consequences.

In 1915, Gandhi returned to India. After the massacre at Jal-

116

*Calcutta: Bridge over the Hooghly, a mouth of the Ganges*

lianwala Bagh, he plunged into action, and started a campaign of nonviolent noncooperation designed to bring the British administration to a standstill. Men, women and children all over India joined him. They gave up their jobs, boycotted legislatures and courts, left government schools and colleges, again refused to buy British goods and, in spite of police beatings and arrests, defied laws that they believed to be wrong. One such law was the tax on salt. Gandhi believed it was wrong to tax salt which even the poorest people needed to use. In 1930, after notifying the viceroy, he and seventy-eight chosen followers marched twenty-four days to a beach where he made salt from sea water to show that the poor could make their own salt without paying a tax. Thousands did likewise. There were not enough jails for all who so disobeyed.

Gandhi had another means of protest. He would go on fast, and the British, knowing how powerful his influence was, would not dare to let him die. He fasted also to influence his own people. To be free, he saw that Indians would have to change some of their ways, too, especially the discrimination of the caste system. He once fasted for three weeks until he was assured that the Untouchables, those he called Children of God, would get better treatment. Rioting between Hindus and Muslims distressed him and he went on fast many times to make them stop.

Gandhi had the strong support of the masses of the people be-

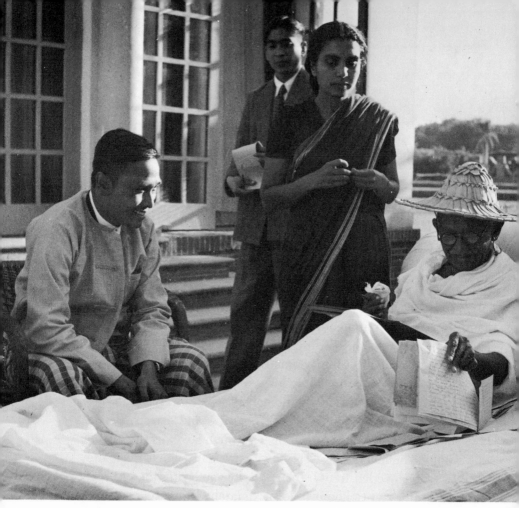

*Gandhi, 1947. His visitor is the Prime Minister of Burma.*

cause he went to the villages where most Indians live and involved them in the struggle for freedom. He took up spinning cotton thread and weaving the rough homespun cloth called *khadi* that Indians could wear instead of spending money on fabrics from abroad, and he encouraged cottage industries to supply all domestic needs. The spinning wheel, called a *charka*, is on the national flag.

Some of the well-to-do Indian nationalist leaders in the towns did not find it easy at first to follow Gandhi's example of such extremely simple living. Among them was his great friend, Motilal Nehru, father of Prime Minister Jawaharlal Nehru and grand-

father of Prime Minister Indira Gandhi. (Mrs. Gandhi is Jawaharlal Nehru's daughter. She married Feroze Gandhi, not related
to the Mahatma.) Motilal had in many respects admired the
British and had enjoyed a comfortable living under their administration. He had been a leader of the Indian National Congress
from the beginning, hoping reform could be accomplished with
the collaboration of the British. But when Gandhi was thrown
into prison, Motilal and all his family made a bonfire of their
handsome foreign clothes, and changed to *khadi*. They also spent
months, even years, in jail. So did many other leaders, especially
during World War II. Indeed, when the government of free India
was finally formed, it was almost a club of those who had been in
prison.

During World War II, a "Quit India" movement swept the
country and the British knew they would have to yield. But there
was the terrible problem of the growing friction between the
Muslim and Hindu sections of the population. The Muslims num-
bered over ninety million or nearly one quarter of the people of
India and were the majority in five provinces, including two of
the largest, the Punjab and Bengal. The Muslim League was led
by Mohammed Ali Jinnah, a lawyer who had been prominent in
the Congress Party before Gandhi. Jinnah did not want a minority
position in a national state but, instead, a separate homeland for
the Muslims. Gandhi and the Congress wanted a united India,
with freedom for all religions. Jinnah prevailed. In 1947, the
British transferred the power to two independent countries, still
nominally within the British Commonwealth. The largest area of
Pakistan was to the west in the Punjab and Sind. But East Bengal,
between Calcutta and Assam, much more densely populated, also
was made part of Pakistan.* Most of India lies between.

The transfer of power did not occur without bitter fighting
between Hindus and Muslims. As Muslims fled to Pakistan and
Hindus to India, millions were killed on both sides. And so, although India had finally become independent, it was not the
nonviolent or the united India that Gandhi had dreamed of.

---

* Now Bangladesh.            119

While the country was celebrating with fireworks and dancing, he was helping the victims of the rioting between Hindus and Muslims. When riots broke out in Delhi against the Muslims, Gandhi went on another fast to make both sides stop. Gandhi's persistent efforts to protect minorities, especially the Muslims, angered a few fanatic Hindus. At a prayer meeting in a garden in New Delhi, on January 30, 1948, Gandhi (Bapu or father he was lovingly called by his people) was shot. Prime Minister Nehru said then: "A light has gone out of our lives and there is darkness everywhere. And yet I am wrong for the light that shone . . . was no ordinary light. It will illuminate this country for many years, and a thousand years later it will be seen and it will give solace to innumerable hearts. For that light represented something more than the immediate present; it represented the living truth, the eternal truth, reminding us of the right path . . . taking this ancient country to freedom."

# 13
## Independent India

January 26 is Republic Day in India. It commemorates the adoption of the Constitution, twenty years to the day after Gandhi and Jawaharlal Nehru had pledged that India would be free. New Delhi then is cool and bright with flowers. People from all over India come to the capital to watch or take part in parades, displays of folk dancing, and other celebrations which go on for three days. The closing ceremony is Beating Retreat at the top of the Mall, in front of the President's House. Before packed grandstands, the President arrives in a horse-drawn carriage under the red and gold parasol symbolizing authority, as it did for princes of old. He is escorted by his mounted Bodyguard in their smart red jackets and gold and white turbans, horses prancing, standards flying. Bands from different regiments play and march in intricate formation. One band consists of seventy-five bagpipers in white gaiters, tartans, and red hats with cockades or red turbans, and a corps of drummers with leopard skins hanging from their shoulders. Meanwhile, the camel corps stands at attention on the ramparts of the palace, outlined against the sinking sun. Just before sunset, the bands, five hundred in all, come together to play, very quietly, one of Gandhi's favorite hymns, "Abide With Me." The flags are lowered to the roll of the drums. Then, after the national anthem, the President and his Bodyguard ride briskly back to the Rashtrapati Bhavan. The ceremony is the pride of a great new nation which, at the same time, continues an age-long culture.

121

*Beating Retreat, January 29th*

The Republic of India is a federation of states under a parliamentary government. The executive branch consists of the President, the Vice President, and a Council of Ministers, of whom the Prime Minister, the leader of the majority party, is the real head of government. He (or she) remains in power as long as the administration is supported by the Lok Sabha (House of the People), the lower House of Parliament, to which the Prime Minister and ministers are jointly responsible and of which they must all be members.

The President, the head of state, is elected for five years by the members of both Houses of Parliament and by the Legislative Assemblies of the states. His presidential duties are largely ceremonial except in certain circumstances, when power reverts to that office. Governors of the states, appointed by the President, are also mainly ceremonial, but may exercise some discretionary powers. The political leader of each state is its Chief Minister, who is responsible to the state legislature. Union territories are governed by the President, usually through an administrator.

The Lok Sabha is elected every five years, unless Parliament is dissolved sooner, at a general election in which citizens twenty-one years and over are entitled to vote. Seats are allotted to each state and union territory according to population. In 1977 there were 544 members.

The upper House, the Rajya Sabha (Council of State), is allowed not more than 250 members. Twelve are nominated by the President, for literary, artistic, social or scientific achievement. Others represent the states and union territories. Representatives are elected by the Legislative Assemblies of the states. The Rajya Sabha is not subject to dissolution. One third of its members retire every second year.

*Parliament House, New Delhi*

Parliament meets in a circular red sandstone building below the President's House. At the other end of the Mall is the Supreme Court, the final interpreter of the Constitution and of the rights it guarantees.

India is the world's most populous democracy. For the 1977 general election 193,953,000 men and women went to the polls. Because many Indians do not read or write the ballots show pic-

*Village Panchayat*

tures or symbols for the different parties and candidates. One
party may be represented by a bullock, another by a plough, another by a clay lamp. In fact, electing leaders at the local level is
not new in India. For centuries villages have been administered
by councils of five, called Panchayats (panch = five), chosen by the
villagers. This tradition of local self-government has been continued through a system of Panchayati Raj for the villages and by
municipal corporations and councils in the cities and towns.

In 1947 Jawaharlal Nehru, leader of the then overwhelmingly
popular Congress party, became independent India's first Prime
Minister. He held that office until his death in 1964. Before that,
as noted, he had worked closely with Gandhi and, like him, was
often put in jail by the British. Yet his bonds with England remained very strong. Educated at Harrow and Cambridge, he
spoke and wrote beautiful English—his family teased him because
he spoke Hindi with a slight English accent. While in prison in
1936 he wrote his *Autobiography* and, during World War II, *The
Discovery of India*, a history mixed with personal observations.
He described himself as a man of two cultures, East and West.
He was an internationalist, but he was, above all, an Indian, pas-

124

sionately devoted to the welfare of his people. In India he was called Panditji—ji is added to a name as a sign of affection and respect. In his will Nehru wrote: "I have received so much love and affection from the Indian people that nothing I can do can repay even a small fraction of it and, indeed, there can be no repayment of so precious a thing as affection . . ." When he died, his ashes were scattered, as he wished, in many places so that "they might become an indistinguishable part of India."

Nehru traveled constantly throughout India. Ignorance and poverty distressed him and he was determined that, in free India, living conditions would be better. He was also determined that parliamentary democracy would work. To that end he was frequently in Parliament, leading and stimulating debate. His day was long. Early in the morning, when he was in Delhi, he would be at home to callers who would come with their worries and complaints or merely to greet him, and he was often at his desk until late at night. In between he somehow managed to go to exhibitions, performances and schools to encourage activities of all kinds, for he had many interests. Film stars, mountain climbers,

*Prime Minister Nehru inspecting the Roosevelt House, New Delhi*

writers, young people and world leaders were welcome at his house. He especially enjoyed being with and doing things for children. Sometimes he would put on leather gloves to box with the tiger cubs he kept in a large cage in his garden, or he would watch his shy baby pandas. Wherever Panditji went, crowds lined the roads and submerged him with garlands which he impatiently put aside, anxious to get on with whatever had to be done. On his desk was a bronze cast of Abraham Lincoln's hand, a strong hand which he felt gave him strength, and Robert Frost's lines: "But I have promises to keep, and miles to go before I sleep."

Independence brought partition, the splitting up of the subcontinent into two nations, India and Pakistan, and with it misery for both. In addition to the riots, the massacres and the refugees—Hindus and Sikhs escaping to India and Muslims to Pakistan—there was hunger and general destitution, and thousands died in the streets. Although most of these refugees eventually settled peacefully, tensions continued, especially in border areas and in Kashmir. There was a brief war in 1965 and a second in 1971, when several million people took temporary refuge in India during the bitter struggle between West and East Pakistan, which ended when East Pakistan became Bangladesh. By 1972 both sides began to look for ways to live together in harmony. In 1976 travel restrictions between the two countries were eased, a trickle of trade started, and families separated for decades were able to visit one another. In September 1978, after eighteen years, the Indian cricket team played a match in Pakistan. In these years, also, old problems with Nepal, Bhutan and Bangladesh were resolved, creating a better climate among the countries of the subcontinent.

The Republic of India recognizes all religions. Opportunities are open to all, regardless of faith. Discrimination on religious grounds is illegal. In 1971 India's population of almost 548 million included 453 million Hindus, 61 million Muslims, 14 million Christians, 10 million Sikhs, almost 4 million Buddhists, over 2.5 million Jains, as well as Parsis (followers of Zoroaster, originally from Persia, who settled mainly in Bombay and vicinity), Jews and

*Prime Minister Nehru in Ludhiana to inaugurate Punjab Agricultural University with Ambassador and Mrs. Galbraith*

*Nehru relaxing*

others. India's leaders are from every major religion. Two of the first six presidents have been Muslims. There is still, however, a measure of interreligious strife, the legacy of past conflict and hatred.

At Independence, India was not yet one united nation. In addition to the part under direct British rule, British India included about five hundred semi-independent feudal states, ruled locally by their princes. Some of these princes lived lavishly, and the more important, when they came to Delhi, were, like visiting potentates, honored by from nine- to twenty-one-gun salutes. They had to relinquish their political power and privileges and become citizens of the Republic of India. In return they were granted by the government a generous privy purse which enabled them to keep up some of their estates. The amount was to be reduced with succeeding generations. In 1971 these grants were abolished. A few of the princes went into the government, some turned their palaces into hotels. Many are forgotten. In 1979 India was composed of twenty-two states and nine union territories. Further divisions are possible.

With so many regional languages, as different one from another as Icelandic from Greek, it was hard, as we have seen, to find a common national language. Not everyone wanted Hindi even if a majority no longer wanted English. For the south Indian states Hindi is still an alien tongue. The central government continues to use English, although now some Hindi-speaking states submit reports in Hindi and enclose an English translation. There has also been trouble among students. English was important because many essential books, especially in the sciences, had not been translated into Hindi or other Indian languages. At the same time, English was not adequately taught in the schools, so that students were not prepared to use it when they reached the university. More and more books are being translated into Hindi and the other Indian languages, but the task is far from complete. The shift from English has had to proceed slowly.

The greatest problem of all for the new nation has been poverty.

Although India is still relatively poor, important changes are taking place, sometimes rapidly. Those who return to India after an absence of several years notice many more bicycles, scooters, and even cars. Not long ago the only way a villager could get from his village to town was on foot, by bullock- or horse-drawn cart, or on a camel. Train travel was a luxury, and the railway station was often miles distant. Now the well-off man of a village owns a bicycle on which he may also take his wife and children. For government clerks and business employees the scooter is the mark of success. Quite recently, for intercity travel, an improved bus network, following new roads, has been established, linking industrialized areas.

Another prized possession that has become common in India is the transistor radio. It is of special value because it works where there has never been electricity or a telephone or newspapers and extends knowledge and information, as well as providing entertainment.

Television was developed in India in the 1960s by the government, primarily for educational purposes. All radio and television in India is government controlled. Programs now include some entertainment, notably Indian films. At first television was available only in the cities. Gradually, as transmission by satellite is introduced, it can be viewed in villages as well, but so far in only a very small part of the country. The government is providing television sets to some communities and schools which otherwise could not afford them.

In the United States every child must go to school. Until Independence, education in India was largely the privilege of those who could afford it. Most Indians never had the chance to learn to read and write. This did not mean that they were unlearned, for knowledge was transmitted orally, and, because they could not write things down, they had to remember much more, and more carefully. Indians sometimes have remarkable memories. They may know their long epics and sacred texts by heart, merely from hearing them. Today many more Indians go to school—about

*Village school*

*School lunch*

100 million in 1979 as compared with only 23.5 million in 1951. It was estimated in 1979 that 34 percent of all people could read, more than twice the 16 percent for 1950. Literacy is much higher in urban communities than in rural areas and much greater for men than for women. In 1951 only one quarter as many women as men were literate; in 1971 the percentage was a little below half. In 1977 the government launched a massive program of adult education, with the hope of increasing the literacy rate to 65 percent by 1983. This goal is perhaps optimistic, but progress is steady, particularly for women.*

In India men and women have equal rights. Equal opportunities are open to women, and no jobs are barred to them. Indeed, in Manipur, in India's far northeast corner, women have long been the wage earners in control of the family finances; husbands are the dependents. During the struggle for independence, women took an active part and often went to jail along with the men. In the Republic of India women have held prominent positions, including those of governor, ambassador, member of Parliament, cabinet minister, and prime minister. Unlike earlier times, many girls now go to colleges—seven times as many in 1965 as in 1950. As educational opportunities open up for the less advantaged, more and more women are learning how to improve their communities and their way of life.

At present, primary education to the fourth class (ages six to eleven) is free, and it is compulsory in most states. Eighty-seven percent of the children in this age group were in school in 1978, as against 33 percent twenty-five years before. Education is free to age fourteen in all but three states, and in all states to age fourteen for girls and students from underprivileged communities. School attendance is encouraged through school lunch programs, free books and uniforms, rather than by the truant officer.

---

* In the 1971 census, in Kerala and Chandigarh where literacy is highest, approximately 70 percent, it was 76 percent for men and 63 percent for women.

In villages classes are often held out under the trees. If necessary, where there are not enough buildings, they may be held in tents. In remote Jaisalmer, on the edge of Rajasthan, as we were exploring a deserted five-story building that had once belonged to some rich merchants, we came upon a boys' school in session on the roof. The children sat on the floor; their only equipment consisted of a few well-worn books. Even though the classroom and supplies were simple and improvised, there would have been none fifty years ago. There are today many Indian doctors, scientists, and engineers whose parents could not read and write.

Between 1960 and 1977 universities in India increased in number from 45 to 105, each with many affiliated colleges. There were nine times as many university students. While the number of students enrolled in art and science courses quadrupled, by far the greatest increase was in engineering. A sixth of all college students were on scholarship, an indication that higher education is no longer confined to the rich. At the vocational level the government supports thousands of multipurpose schools to train workers for the new industries, and agricultural centers to teach farmers new methods. Village artisans, who sometimes waste their skills on useless objects made of inferior materials, are taught to turn out handicrafts that will sell, and for which the government can help to find a market.

One concern for India has been that able Indian students who have gone abroad for their professional training have stayed away after their studies are completed because they cannot find positions in India to match their professional attainments. This still happens. But now institutes have been established which provide first-rate instruction and facilities for advanced research. One of these is the Indian Institute of Technology (IIT) at Kanpur, started in 1962. In less than a decade it was training most of the computer operators in India and had achieved such high standards in other fields as well that it attracted back some of the best Indian scholars outside India, in this case reversing the "brain drain." There are now in India five national Institutes of Technology, each set up with guidance and aid from abroad, and all contributing significantly to India's development.

Furthermore, India's nuclear energy program, begun in 1944, with the goal of providing electricity for her new industries, agricultural machines and domestic needs, has drawn to it hundreds of Indian nuclear physicists. The first atomic power station, at Tarapur, built by the United States, has provided training for future nuclear engineers. Other Indian scientists, engaged in space research, have already made notable contributions to space technology.

The great expansion of education has caused unrest, especially among graduates unable to find jobs. But one unexpected bonus has been a kind of brain drain that has paid off. As India's newly rich oil-producing neighbors have started their own development, they have discovered in India's vast reserve of technically trained workers the talents they require. Skilled workers have become one of India's most valuable exports. The money they send home has bolstered India's trade balance and has brought marked prosperity,

*Atomic energy—Trombay, near Bombay*

*District agricultural officer, receiving an application for a tube well*

particularly to Kerala, the most literate and once the poorest state, and the one from which many of these workers have been recruited.

When I first visited India, in 1956, most manufactured goods were imported. An inexpensive watch from the United States was a magnificent present; watches were not made in India. Now India is almost completely self-sufficient, not only in consumer goods and basic commodities such as steel and cement but also in the machinery necessary to support her major industries. Out in the country where, thirty, or just five, years ago, there were only villages, you may see dams, generators for electricity, steel mills, fertilizer plants, factories, even a nuclear reactor. The result is more goods in the shops and more farm machinery in the fields, above all in the Punjab, India's most prosperous farmland. Here the tractor has supplanted the wooden plough. Here too nearly all villages have electricity, something which at Independence was virtually unknown in rural India.

In 1963, with Prime Minister Nehru, we attended the inaugura-

*The family tractor goes to town*

tion of the Punjab Agricultural University; it took place in a bungalow out in the fields. Five years later I was invited back to a farmers' fair. I found large brick buildings spread over acres of green campus, and in one courtyard ten thousand farmers listening to a lecture on growing wheat. Large tents housed demonstrations of farm machinery, various kinds of seed, fertilizers, animal husbandry and much else. Some of the farmers had come by bicycle and cart and some by tractor, covered with a shamiana to provide shaded transport for the family. I was witnessing a significant support of the green revolution.

For years after Independence, to avoid starvation, India had to depend on huge shipments of grain from abroad, much of it from the United States. In the late 1970s, in spite of the population growth, India had a reserve of from 15 to more than 20 million tons of food grains and even some for export. Along with chemical, fertilizers, improved planting, better seeds, storage facilities, multiple cropping, and new varieties of wheat and rice, water has been most important in this change. Dams and canals now irrigate millions of once-barren acres. In addition, thousands of tube wells have been drilled, a contrast to the old slow methods of drawing

*Irrigation—old.* ABOVE: *Blindfolded camel.* BELOW: *Walking beam*

*Irrigation—new: note the ramps up which workers carry concrete.*

water—the Persian wheel, turned by bullocks or a blindfolded camel (he won't keep on walking if he can see he isn't going anywhere), or a seesaw arrangement whereby water for irrigation is raised in a bucket by the weight of a man walking up and down a wooden beam. The Rajasthan Canal mentioned earlier has at last begun to make the desert bloom, and transport there has progressed from camelback to camel-drawn carts with enormous rubber tires.

With adequate and dependable water and high-yielding crops, India may finally be overcoming the hardships of drought and famine. Farmers will no longer have to live in tiny huts surrounded by their skinny dogs and children. Instead they will be proud of their lands and their profession and hopeful that they can soon replace their mud houses with ones of baked brick. Some have already done so. Other hazards must still be faced, however. In 1978 vast floods covered much rich agricultural land, the result of years of deforestation by an ever-expanding population. Protection and control of trees are also necessary.

More food and more goods mean longer life. In India life has been truly short. In 1950 a boy could expect to live only to the age of thirty-two. By 1978 life expectancy at birth was fifty-two. That is a big jump but still far less than the life expectancy of seventy-three years in the United States. In India, unlike in the United States, the men live longer than the women.

Modern medicine has checked many diseases. Plague and small-pox have disappeared. Tuberculosis and cholera have been controlled to a degree. With the use of DDT, cases of malaria dropped from 75 million in 1951 to 100,000 in 1965, although this battle is not yet won because a strain of mosquito that is resistant to DDT has evolved.

Better hospitals and centers for medical research offer treatment previously unobtainable in India. The number of hospitals and dispensaries has risen greatly; many more, however, are required before good medical care will be generally available. In an Indian village you don't go down the street to the drugstore if you need an aspirin. The only source of medical supplies is likely to be a simple government-supported clinic-dispensary, one or two concrete rooms furnished with a cot and a medicine cabinet, which may have to serve several villages. One of the early United States Peace Corps volunteers, who had had a first-aid course and some veterinary training, one day cleaned a child's infected foot. He

*Health Center, central India*

was startled to find, every evening thereafter, villagers gathered outside his door and even perched on the compound wall, waiting for him to come home to hand out antiseptics, ointments and Band-Aids. In all that thickly populated neighborhood there was not, at that time, any dispensary.

Although health services are still scarce, there are in India more than twice as many doctors and seven times as many nurses as there were in 1947. Medical colleges have increased in number from 30 to 106. For a long time nursing, like acting, was not considered a profession suitable for girls of good families. But this too is changing, and many dedicated, well-trained young women work long hours in the little clinics in the villages. There are many women doctors as well.

Imaginative projects also make good use of limited medical resources and personnel. Well-staffed traveling clinics are sent to rural areas, a few weeks at a time, to provide medical care not otherwise available. I once visited a mobile hospital, set up in tents, for the treatment of eye diseases. Operations were performed by experienced eye surgeons. In one tent we saw about thirty elderly patients, lying on cots in rows under red blankets, waiting their turns. Throngs of villagers were outside, hoping to be examined and treated before the hospital moved elsewhere.

A major source of disease has been polluted water. Several hundred thousand urban and rural sanitation schemes have been initiated by the government. Now, although many village women still fetch their water from stagnant ponds, it is no longer rare to find a village with a well-regulated water system and women filling their polished jugs from a tap. By 1978, 64,000 villages had been provided with safe drinking water. But 153,000 villages had no source of water within a mile or more. The goal is to assure safe water for all villages by 1981.

To improve housing conditions the Indian government and business firms give subsidies to low-salaried workers so that they can afford adequate accommodations. In New Delhi the central government offers quarters for workers according to their pay. The

*New well, old jugs*

states also support many housing projects. Loans at minimum interest enable individuals who do not have the cash on hand to build. Several thousand villages have had better housing provided for them. Some completely new towns and cities have been constructed, notably Chandigarh, designed by the great French architect Le Corbusier. He designed the setting, too, by creating a large lake at one end of the city, beyond which lie the foothills of the Himalayas.

Yet all these achievements, however remarkable, are just a beginning. While there is no longer general starvation, more than 40 percent, or 290 million Indians, barely subsist. Far too many are unemployed or underemployed. And the population has been rising rapidly—from 361 million in 1951 to an estimated 625 million in 1977, an increase considerably more than the total present population of the entire United States. The increase occurred not only because of the number of births but also because, with better care, babies are not dying as they once did and because Indians live longer. Every year India must feed, house and clothe an additional number of people as large as the total population of Greater New York or Tokyo. This is a huge task for a poor country. If India is ever to arrive at a standard of living free from deprivation and hardship, population control is essential.

The Indian government has recognized this need and, after a slow start, has given the problem of birth control a high priority.* In the 1960s many thousands of family planning centers were set up, contraceptives were distributed and sterilization was encouraged, sometimes with a gift of money or a transistor radio. (Compulsion was tried briefly during the 1975-1977 emergency period but proved politically disastrous.) Now family planning is being combined with maternal health, child care and nutrition programs, and family welfare workers are being trained as multipurpose health workers. Persuasion and education, especially of women, are important, but the most effective inducement to smaller families, it has been discovered, is improvement in living conditions. Parents must be convinced that, with better health care, they need no longer have many children so that one or two will survive to look after them in their old age. For the very poor, each child represents additional labor and family support. After a certain standard of living has been reached, parents can see the advantages of a small family. This has been demonstrated in Bombay and, most recently, in Kerala, where the birthrate has dropped sharply.

The early 1970s were a time of particular frustration in India. Rising prices, food shortages, adulteration of foods, black marketeering, student unrest, strikes, and charges of corruption were constantly in the news. I remember a roadside billboard outside Calcutta which exhorted everyone, "Tighten your belt. It's the belt of your country." Looking at the people, one wondered how this could be done. Then, on June 26, 1975, Prime Minister Indira Gandhi, hard pressed, declared an emergency, which gave her

---

* The amount budgeted to family planning in 1978 was 4.97 billion rupees, as against 1.4 million rupees in 1952.

*Future Prime Minister and Guest*

authoritarian power. Her opponents were arrested, fundamental rights suspended, the courts and Parliament made compliant, the press censored. Some things changed. Strikes ceased, workers got to their jobs on time, students studied. Favorable monsoons yielded record harvests and so prices stabilized. But the police were also busy, and people feared to speak freely. Indians did not take the loss of their liberties lightly. In January 1977, Mrs. Gandhi called a General Election for March, in which she was defeated, and with her the Congress Party, for the first time since Independence.

The Republic of India is now thirty years old. The associates and followers of Gandhi and Nehru who are still alive and active are that much older. A new generation, which has never lived under British rule, has come of age; one for whom the struggle

*"I wandered over the Himalayas, which are closely connected with old myth and legend, and which have influenced so much of our thought and literature... and I saw there not only the life and vigour and beauty of the present, but also the memoried loveliness of ages past."*
*Jawaharlal Nehru,* DISCOVERY OF INDIA

for Independence and even Nehru himself are already history. Whereas in the beginning the Congress Party had no opposition, gradually other parties emerged, and Congress itself split into factions. These groups, dissatisfied with the emergency restrictions, combined in 1977 to bring in a government headed by the Janata Party, with Morarji Desai, then 81, an influential minister in post-Independence cabinets, as Prime Minister. In August 1979, this uneasy alliance gave way to further coalitions and alignments, under a caretaker Prime Minister, until a new General Election

143

was held in January 1980. Then Mrs. Gandhi and her Congress Party I (I=Indira) won a landslide victory, sweeping into Parliament many young members who had not served before. Thus, despite many problems and challenges, change in Indian political leadership has so far been accomplished by free elections within a democratic framework, as Nehru resolved.

This then is the picture of modern India, a mid-twentieth-century republic and one of the oldest civilizations on earth. The way ahead is not easy. But as India develops her vast industrial, agricultural and, above all, human resources, Indians will have reason to hope that in their country there will be enough to eat, that their children will live to grow up in freedom, with the means to earn a decent living, and that the old will die in peace. In the days of Akbar the Great, remembered as a Golden Age, prosperity depended on the whim of the emperor. Those who were out of favor were out of fortune, or worse. Fortunes still vary. But now the Indian people are their own masters, and the prosperity they seek can bring benefits to all.

# Bibliography

Basham, A. L. *The Wonder That Was India*. New York: Grove Press Inc., 1954.

Bernier, François. *Travels in the Mogul Empire*. Revised edition, based on Irving Brock's translation, by Archibald Constable. London, 1891.

Embassy of India, Washington, D.C. *India: A Nation on the March*. Washington, D.C.: Ex-Speed-Ite Service, 1979.

Festing, Gabrielle. *When Kings Rode to Delhi*. Edinburgh and London: Blackwood & Sons, 1923.

Fodor, Eugene and Curtis, William, editors. *Fodor's Guide to India*. New York - The Hague - Tokyo. Fodor's Modern Guides, Inc., 1962.

Hambly, Gavin. Photographs Wim Swaan. *Cities of Mughul India*. New York: G. P. Putnam's Sons, 1968.

Majumdar, R. C., Raychaudhuri, H. C., and Datta, Kalikinkar. *An Advanced History of India*. London: Macmillan & Co., Ltd., 1946.

Mehta, Rama. *The Life of Keshav, a Family Story from India*. New York: McGraw-Hill Book Company, 1969.

Ministry of Information and Broadcasting. *India Today, Basic Facts*. New Delhi: The Caxton Press Private Ltd., 1969.

Ministry of Information and Broadcasting, Government of India, The Research and Reference Division. *India*. A Reference Annual 1968. New Delhi: The Director, Publications Division, Patiala House, Ministry of Information and Broadcasting, December, 1968.

Ministry of Information and Broadcasting, Government of India, The Research and Reference Division. *India: A Reference Annual 1977–78*. New Delhi: The Director, Publications Division, Patiala House, Ministry of Information and Broadcasting, 1978.

Mukerjee, Professor L. *History of India*. 29th edition. 3 vols. Calcutta: Mondal Brothers & Co., Private Ltd.

Murray, John, *A Handbook for Travellers in India, Pakistan, Burma and Ceylon*. 18th edition. Edited by Sir Arthur C. Lothian. London: John Murray (Publishers) Ltd., 1959. (First edition 1859).

Nehru, Jawaharlal. *The Discovery of India*. Bombay: P. S. Jayasinghe, Asia Publishing House, 1961.

Randhawa, Mohinder Singh and Galbraith, John Kenneth. *Indian Painting: The Scene, Themes and Legends*. Boston: Houghton Mifflin Company, 1968.

Rowland, Benjamin. *The Art and Architecture of India*. Baltimore, Maryland: Penguin Books, 1953.

Woodruff, Philip. *The Men Who Ruled India*. Volume I, *The Founders*, 1953. Volume II, *The Guardians*, 1954. London: Jonathan Cape Limited.

# Index